The Misadventures of
SALEM HYDE

2

Big Birthday Bash
Frank Cammuso

AMULET BOOKS
NEW YORK

Hardcover ISBN: 978-1-4197-1025-4
Paperback ISBN: 978-1-4197-1026-1

Text and illustrations copyright © 2014 Frank Cammuso
Book design by Frank Cammuso and Sara Corbett

Printed and bound in China
10 9 8 7 6 5 4 3 2 1

Amulet Books are available at special discounts when purchased in quantity for premiums and promotions as well as fundraising or educational use. Special editions can also be created to specification. For details, contact specialsales@abramsbooks.com or the address below.

THE ART OF BOOKS SINCE 1949
115 West 18th Street
New York, NY 10011
www.abramsbooks.com

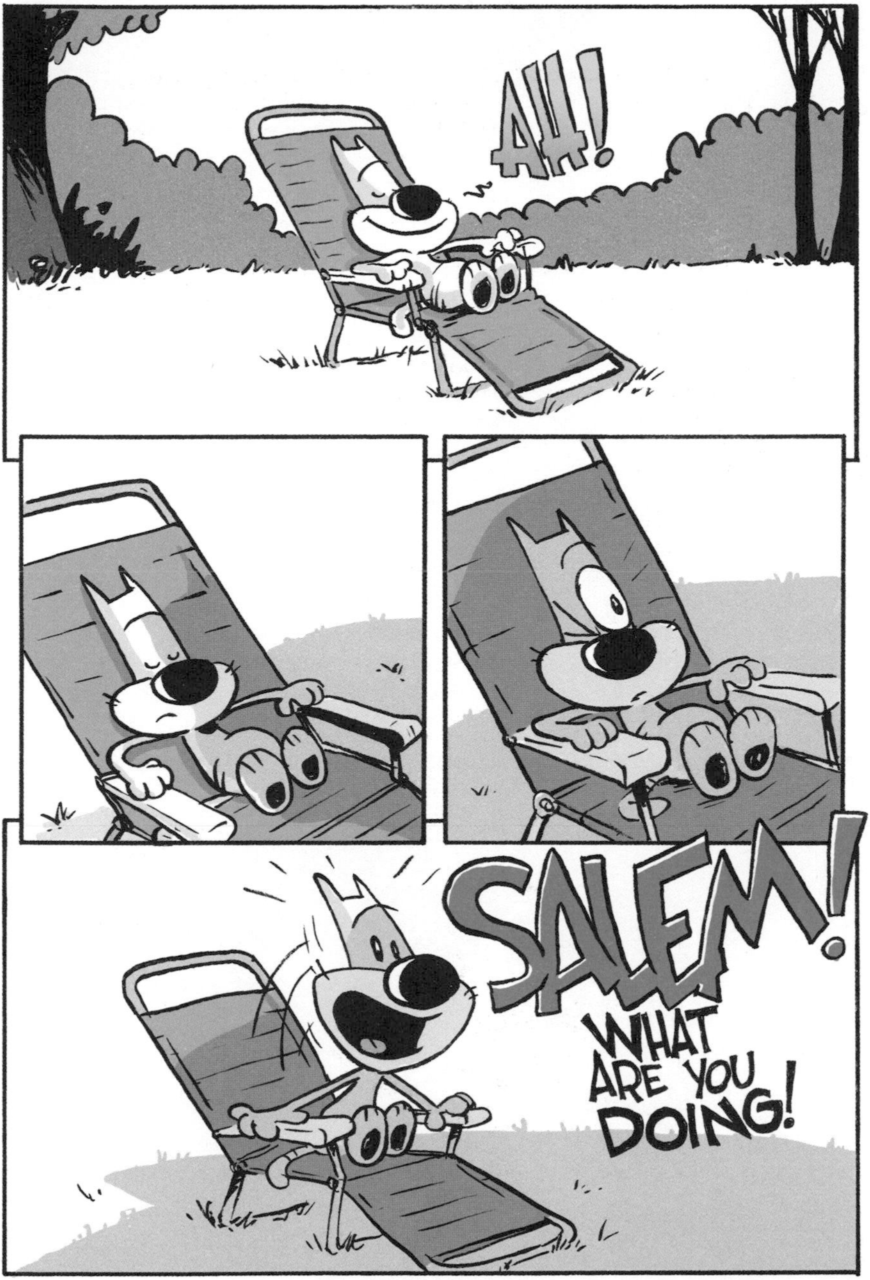
AH!
SALEM!
WHAT ARE YOU DOING!

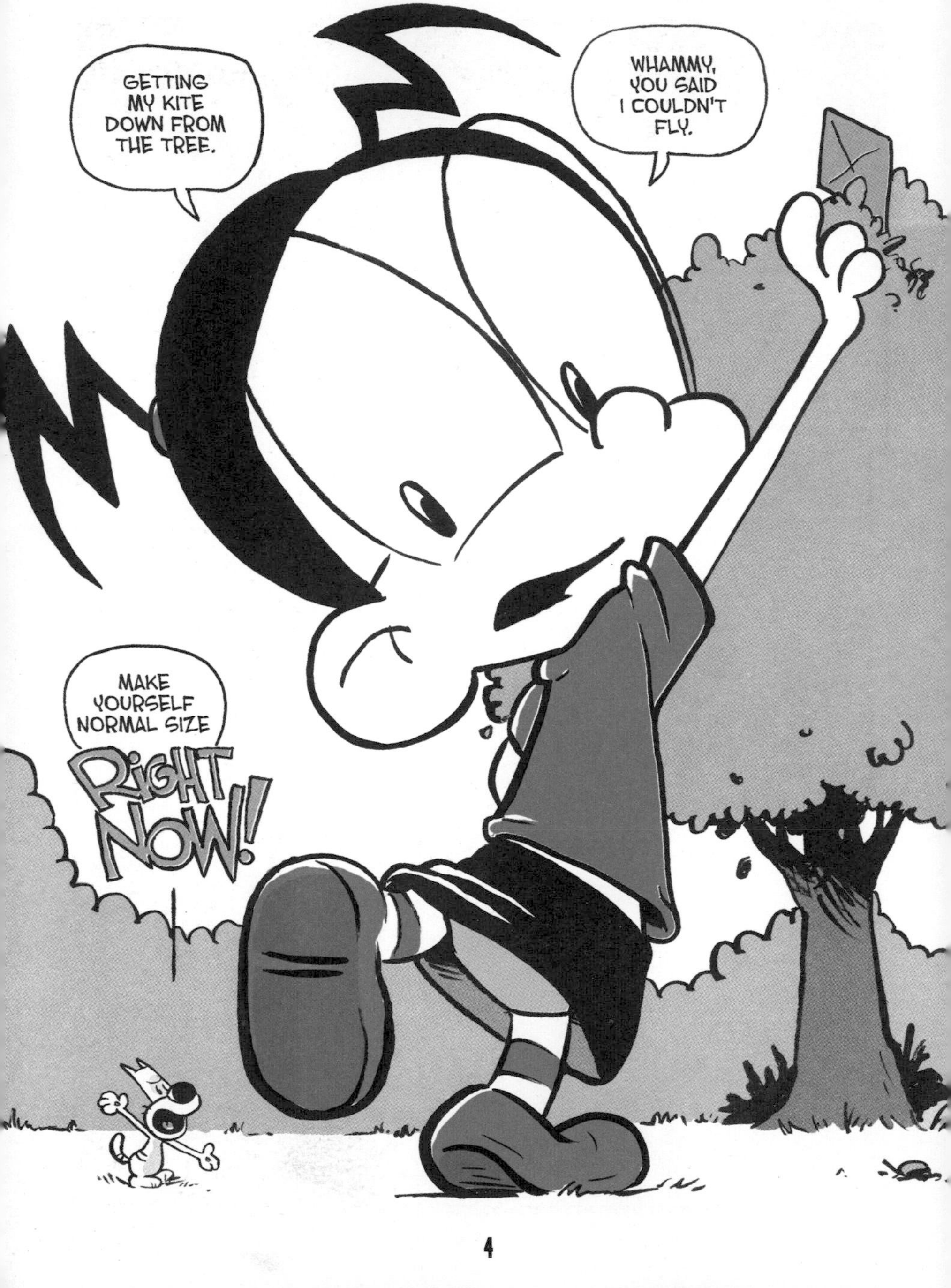
GETTING MY KITE DOWN FROM THE TREE.
WHAMMY, YOU SAID I COULDN'T FLY.
MAKE YOURSELF NORMAL SIZE
RIGHT NOW!

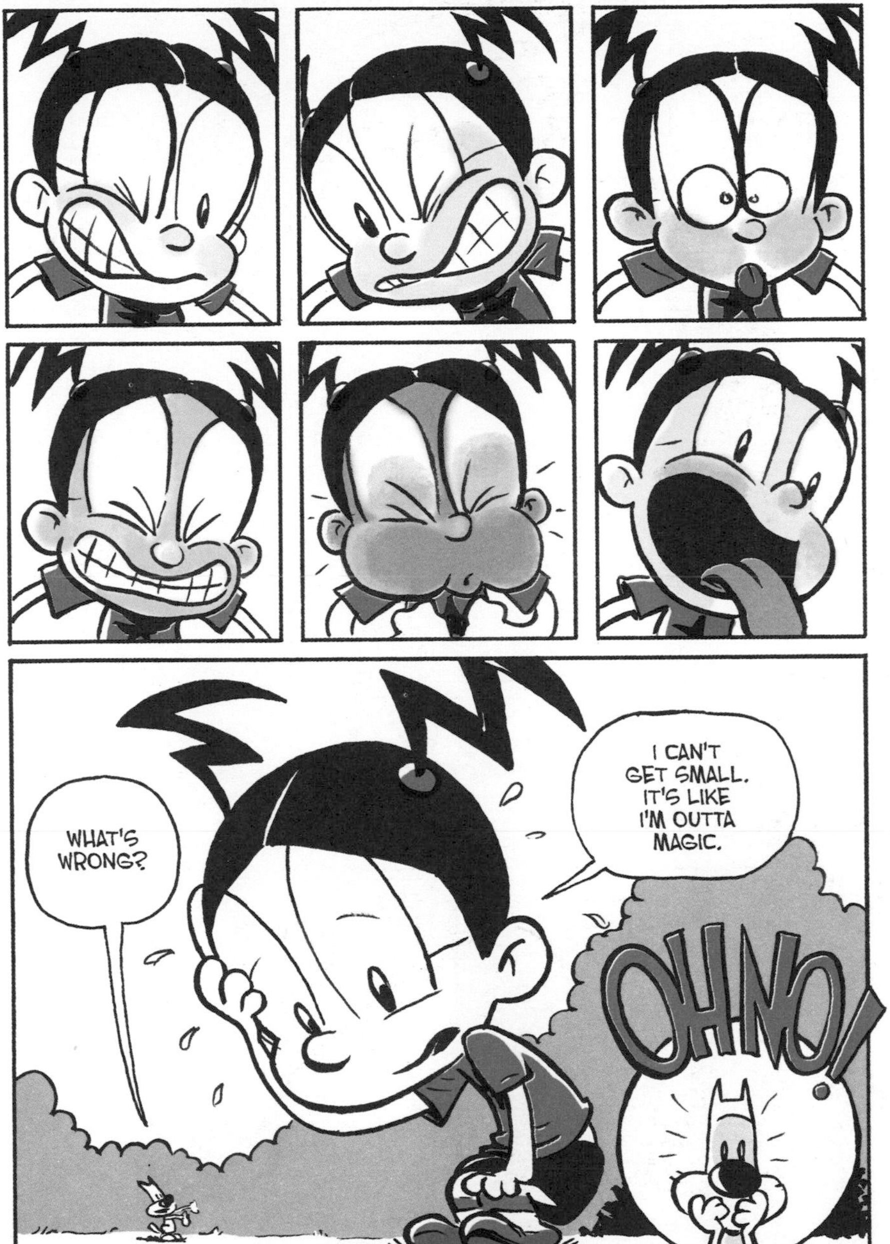
WHAT'S WRONG?
I CAN'T GET SMALL. IT'S LIKE I'M OUTTA MAGIC.
OH NO!

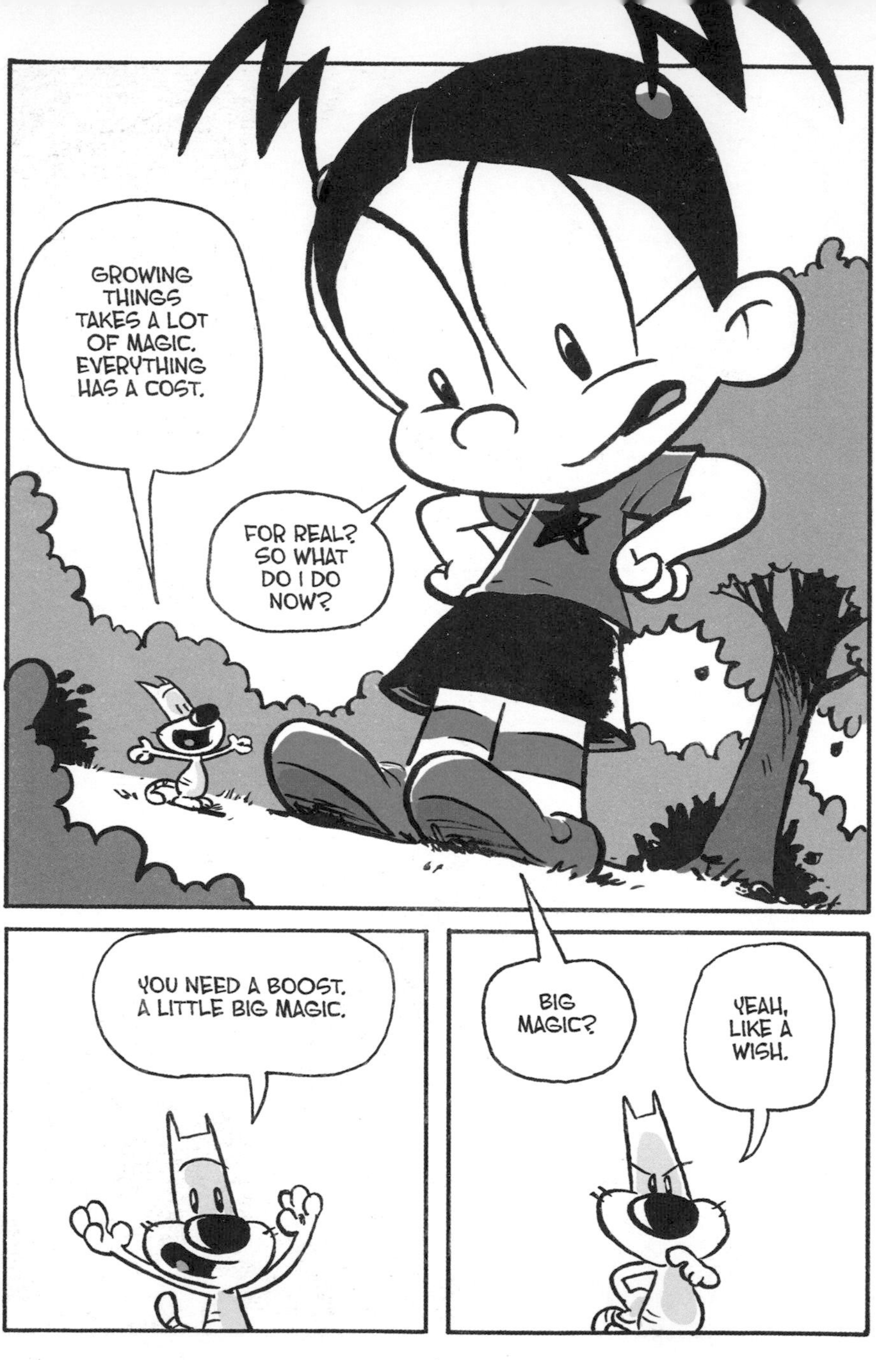
GROWING THINGS TAKES A LOT OF MAGIC. EVERYTHING HAS A COST.
FOR REAL? SO WHAT DO I DO NOW?
YOU NEED A BOOST. A LITTLE BIG MAGIC.
BIG MAGIC?
YEAH, LIKE A WISH.

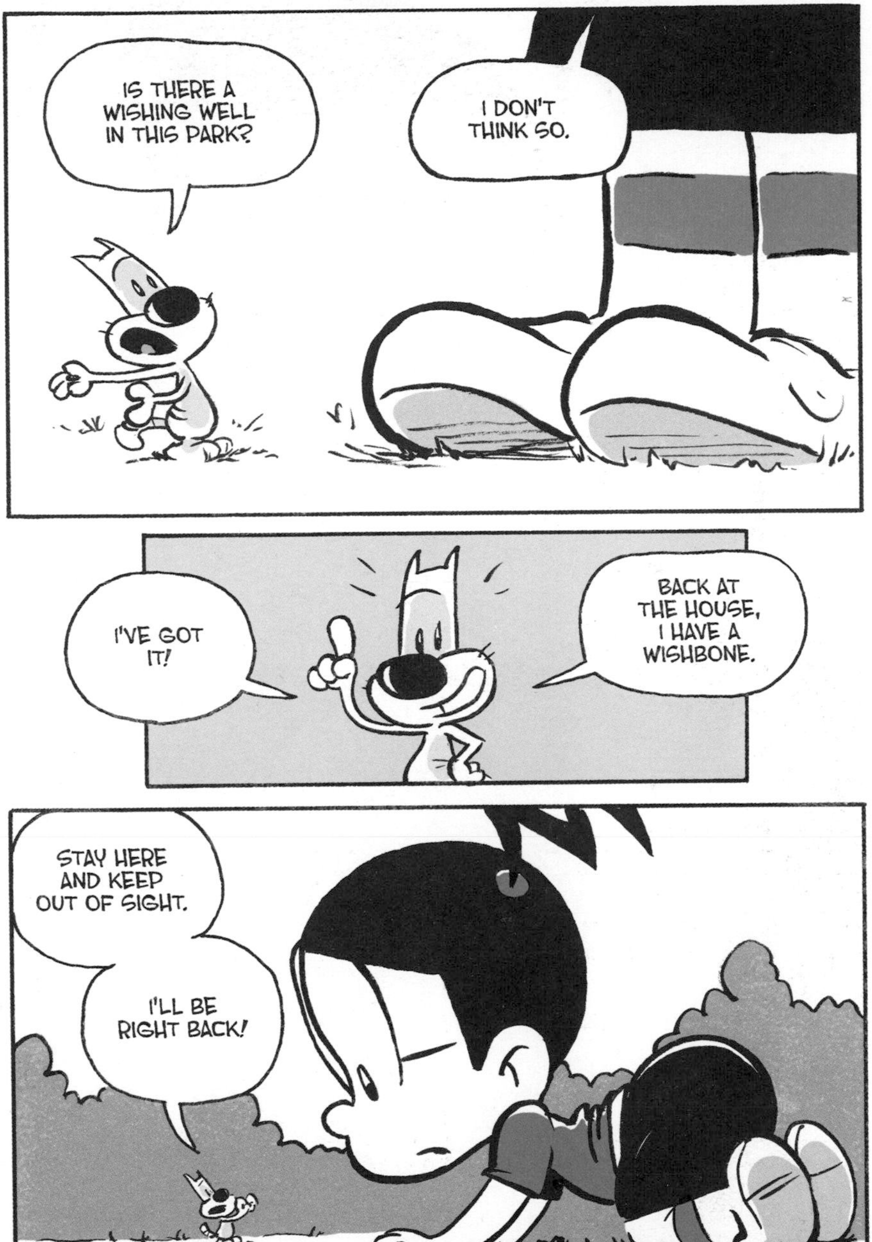
IS THERE A WISHING WELL IN THIS PARK?
I DON'T THINK SO.
I'VE GOT IT!
BACK AT THE HOUSE, I HAVE A WISHBONE.
STAY HERE AND KEEP OUT OF SIGHT.
I'LL BE RIGHT BACK!

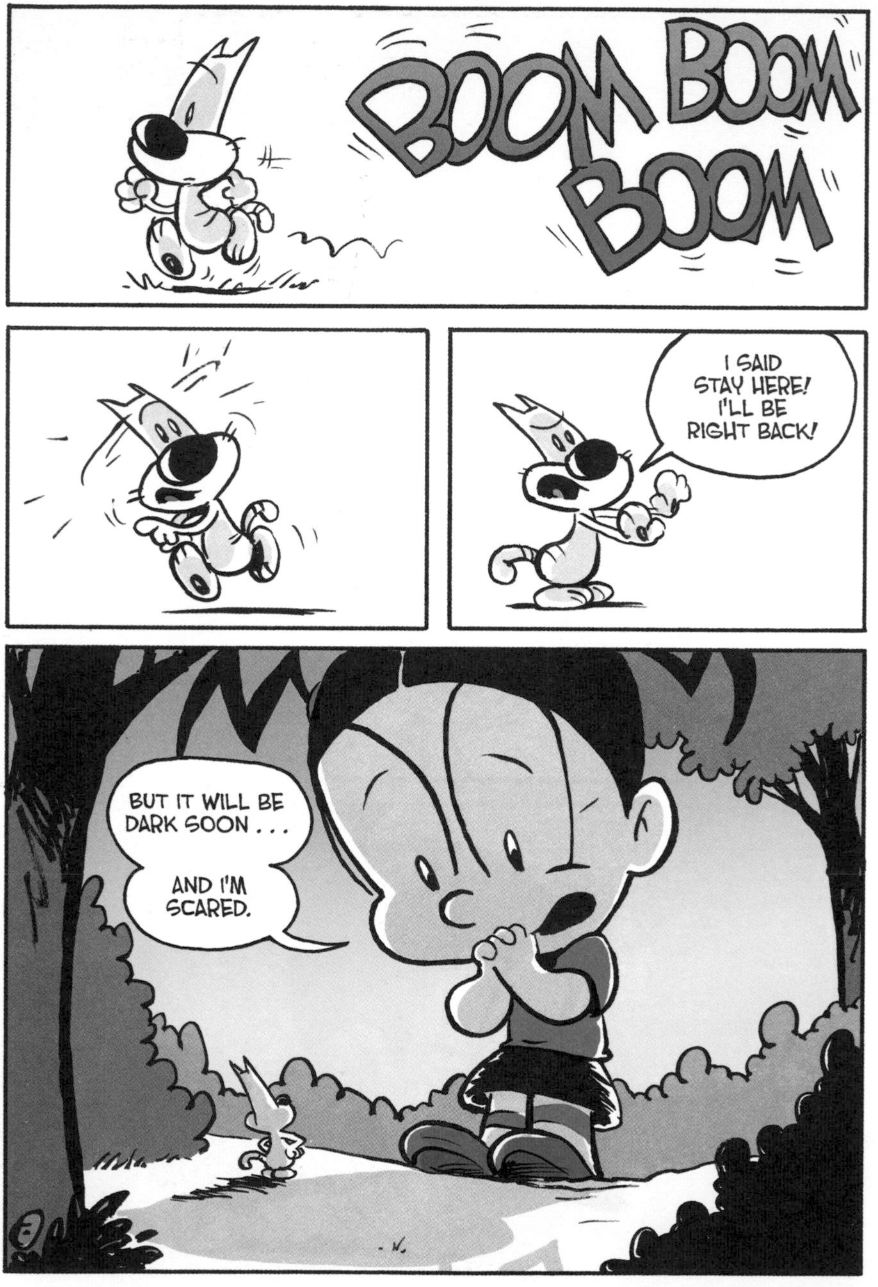
BOOM BOOM BOOM
I SAID STAY HERE! I'LL BE RIGHT BACK!
BUT IT WILL BE DARK SOON . . .
AND I'M SCARED.

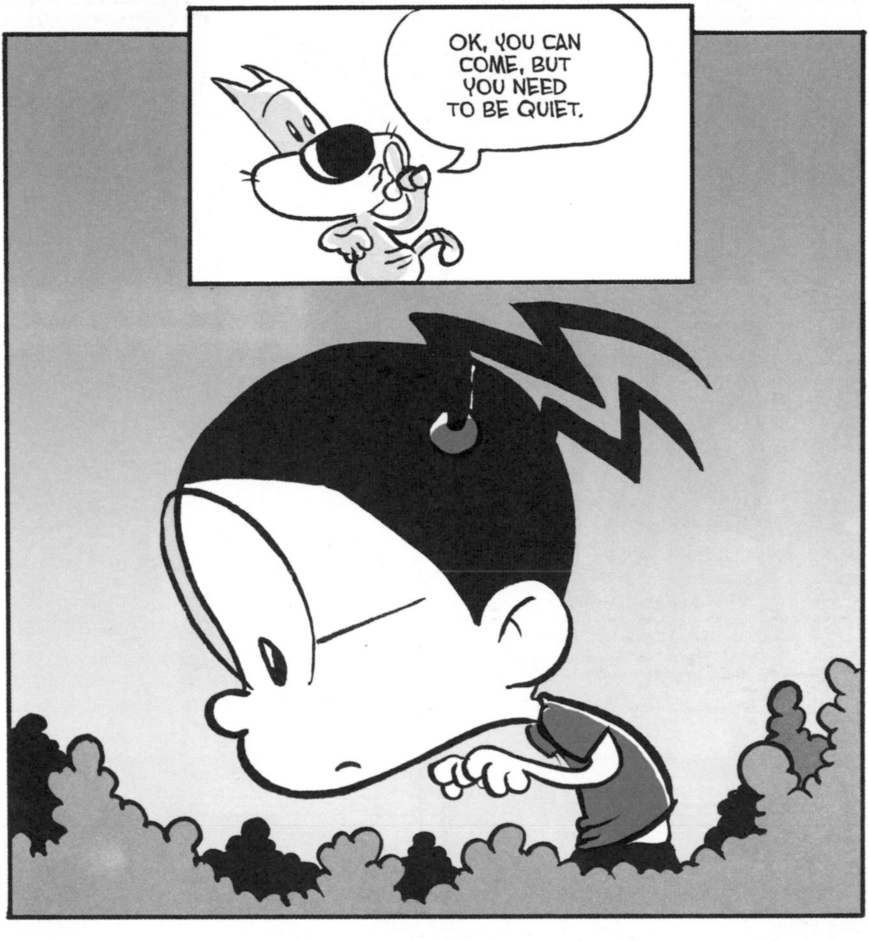
OK, YOU CAN COME, BUT YOU NEED TO BE QUIET.

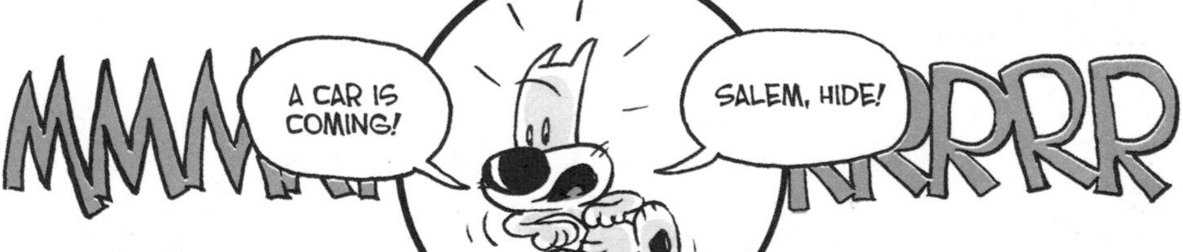
A CAR IS COMING!
SALEM, HIDE!

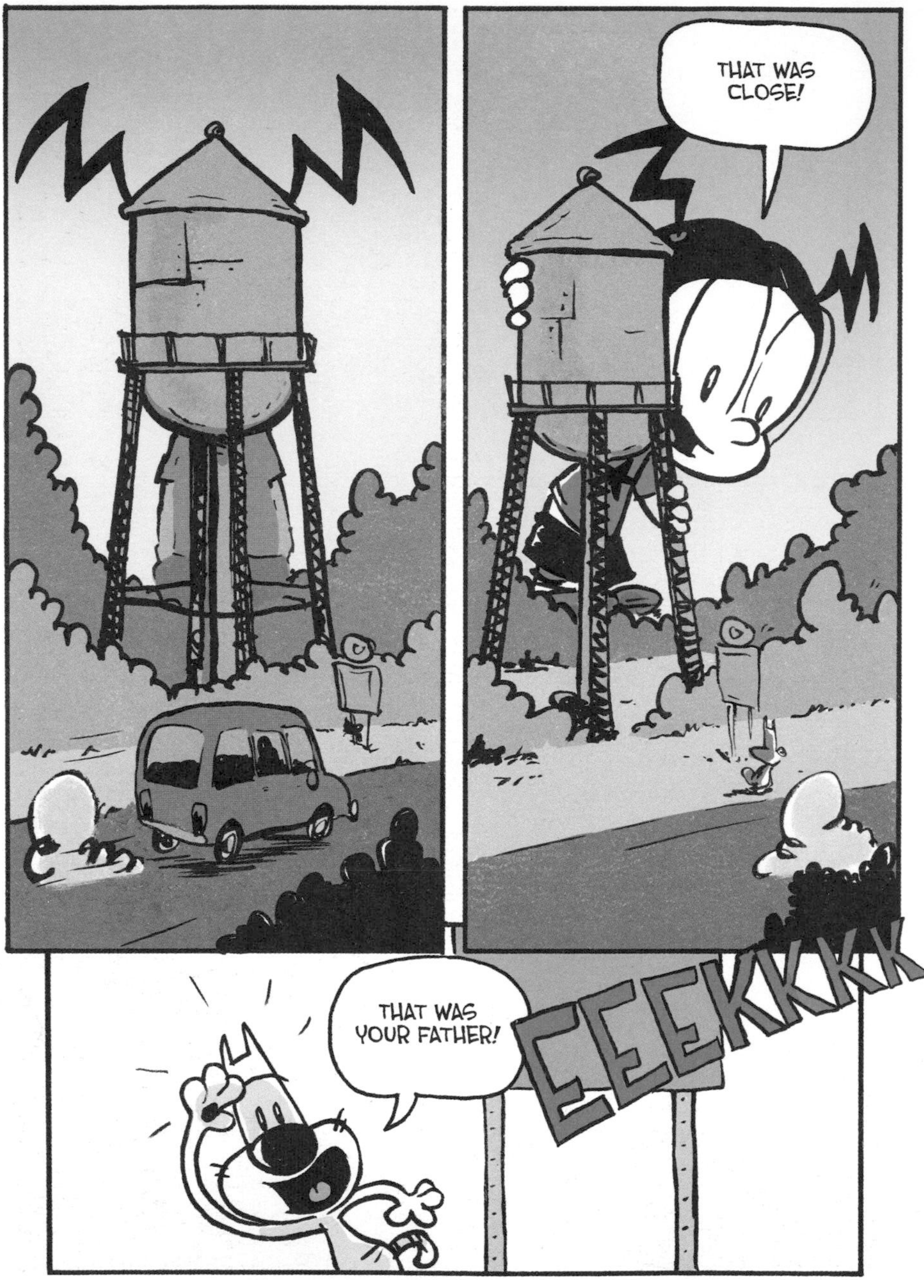
THAT WAS CLOSE!
THAT WAS YOUR FATHER!
EEEKKKK

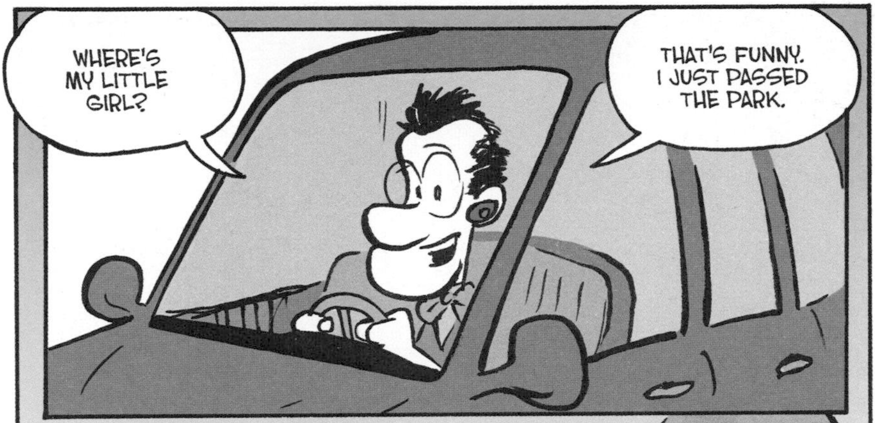
WHERE'S MY LITTLE GIRL?
THAT'S FUNNY. I JUST PASSED THE PARK.
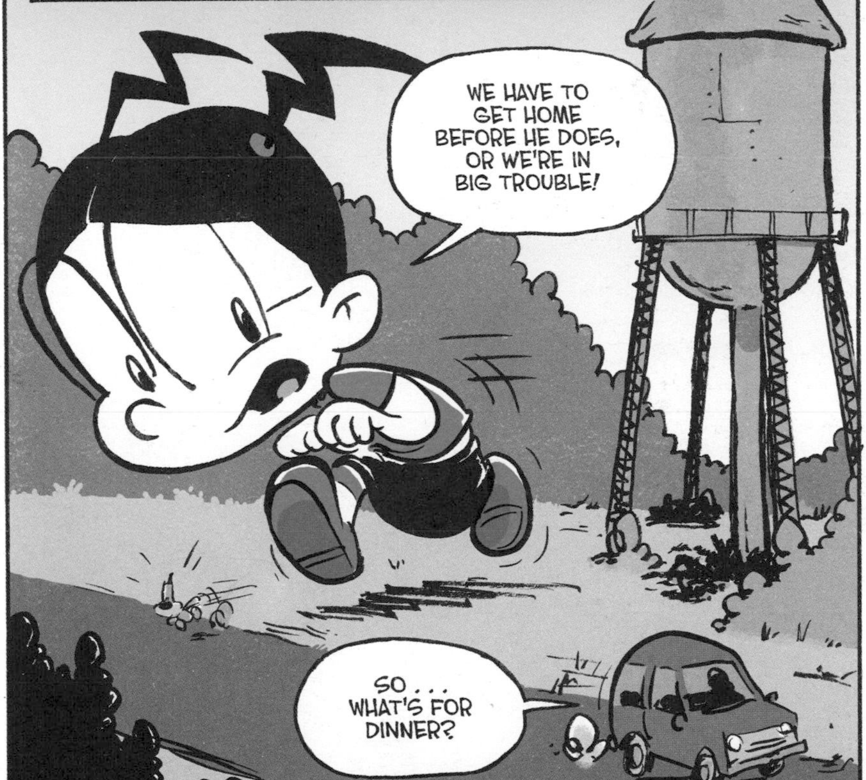
WE HAVE TO GET HOME BEFORE HE DOES, OR WE'RE IN BIG TROUBLE!
SO . . . WHAT'S FOR DINNER?

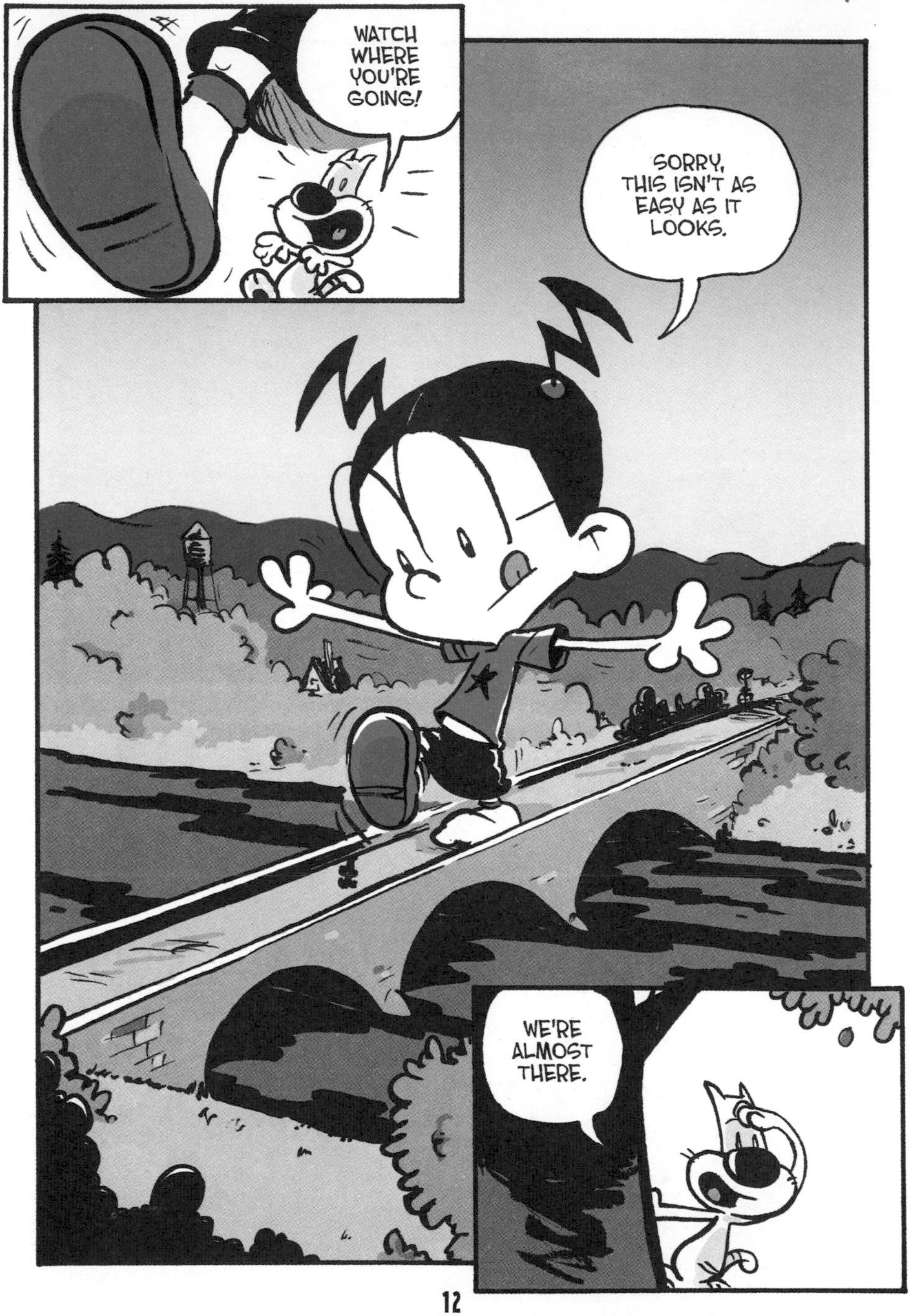
WATCH WHERE YOU'RE GOING!
SORRY, THIS ISN'T AS EASY AS IT LOOKS.
WE'RE ALMOST THERE.

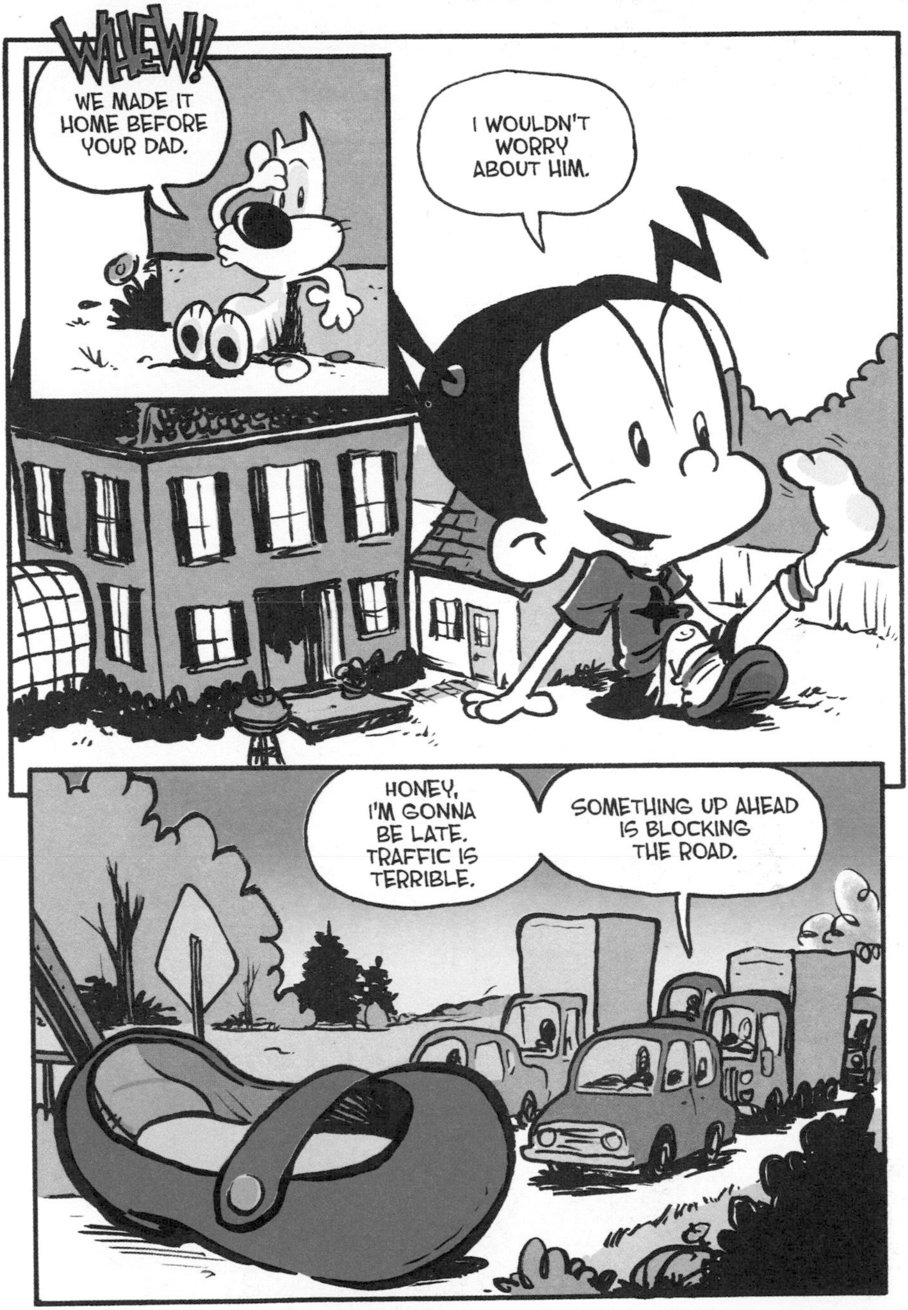
WHEW!
WE MADE IT HOME BEFORE YOUR DAD.
I WOULDN'T WORRY ABOUT HIM.
HONEY, I'M GONNA BE LATE. TRAFFIC IS TERRIBLE.
SOMETHING UP AHEAD IS BLOCKING THE ROAD.

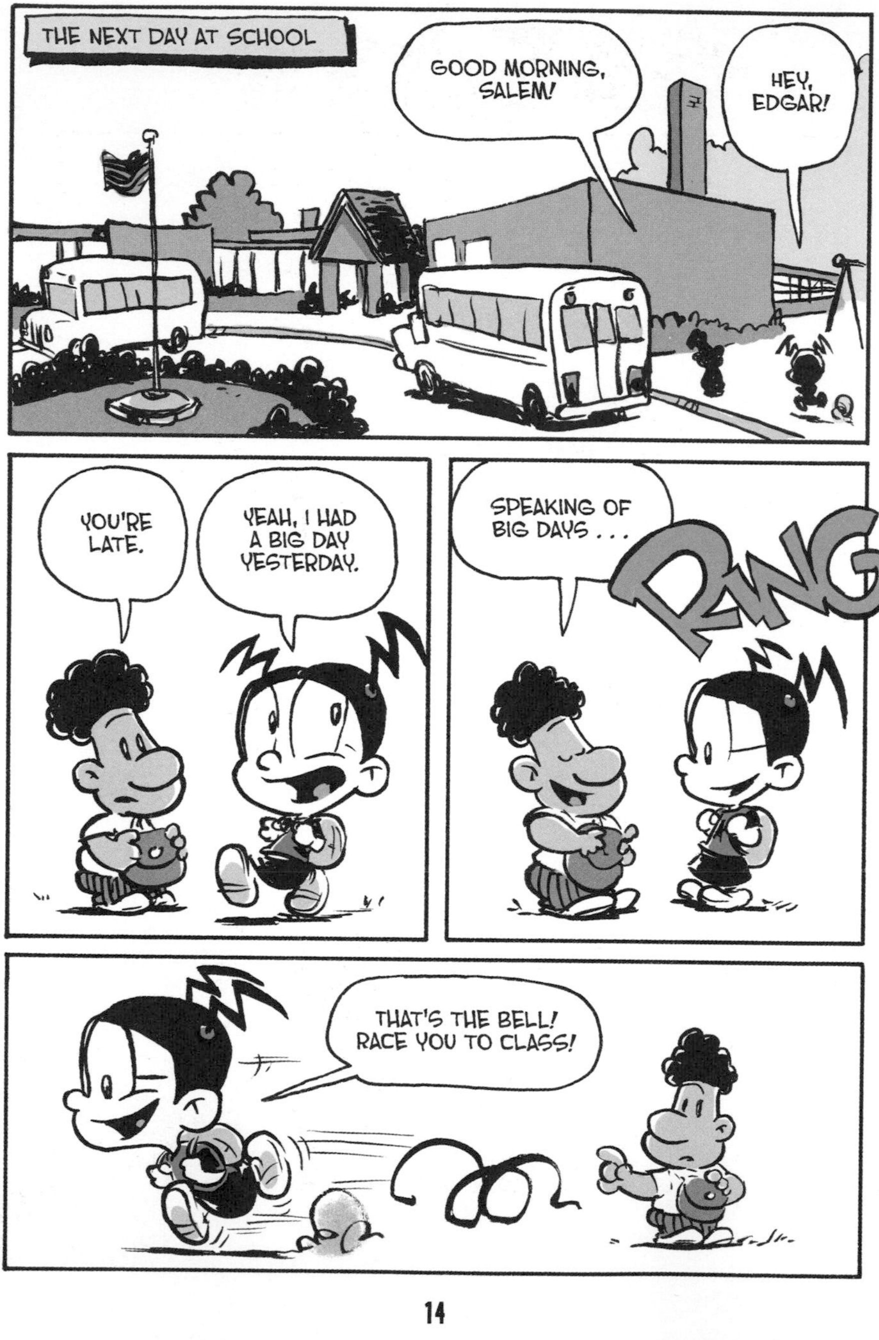
THE NEXT DAY AT SCHOOL
GOOD MORNING, SALEM!
HEY, EDGAR!
YOU'RE LATE.
YEAH, I HAD A BIG DAY YESTERDAY.
SPEAKING OF BIG DAYS . . .
RNG
THAT'S THE BELL! RACE YOU TO CLASS!

Getting to Know Edgar

EDGAR LIKES . . .
1. BIG PARTIES
2. CHEESE DOODLES
3. EVERYONE

EDGAR DISLIKES . . .
1. BIG BULLIES
2. GYM CLASS
3. LIMA BEANS
(WHO CAN BLAME HIM?)

POWERS

EDGAR DOESN'T REALLY HAVE ANY POWERS, BUT HE IS SUPER NICE. (WHICH GOES A LONG WAY THESE DAYS.)
DOES NEVER MISSING A DAY OF SCHOOL COUNT AS A POWER?

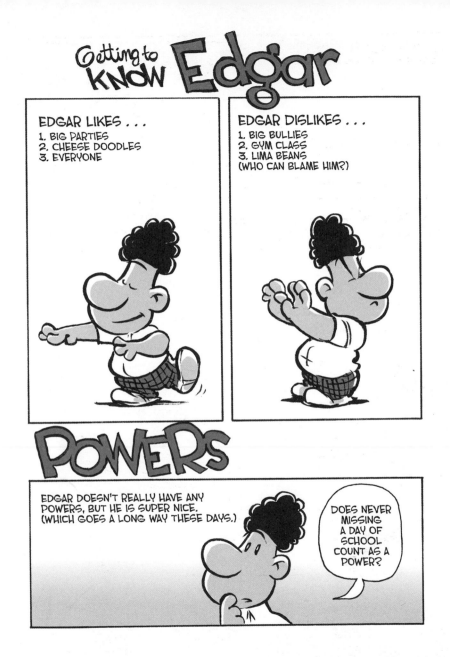

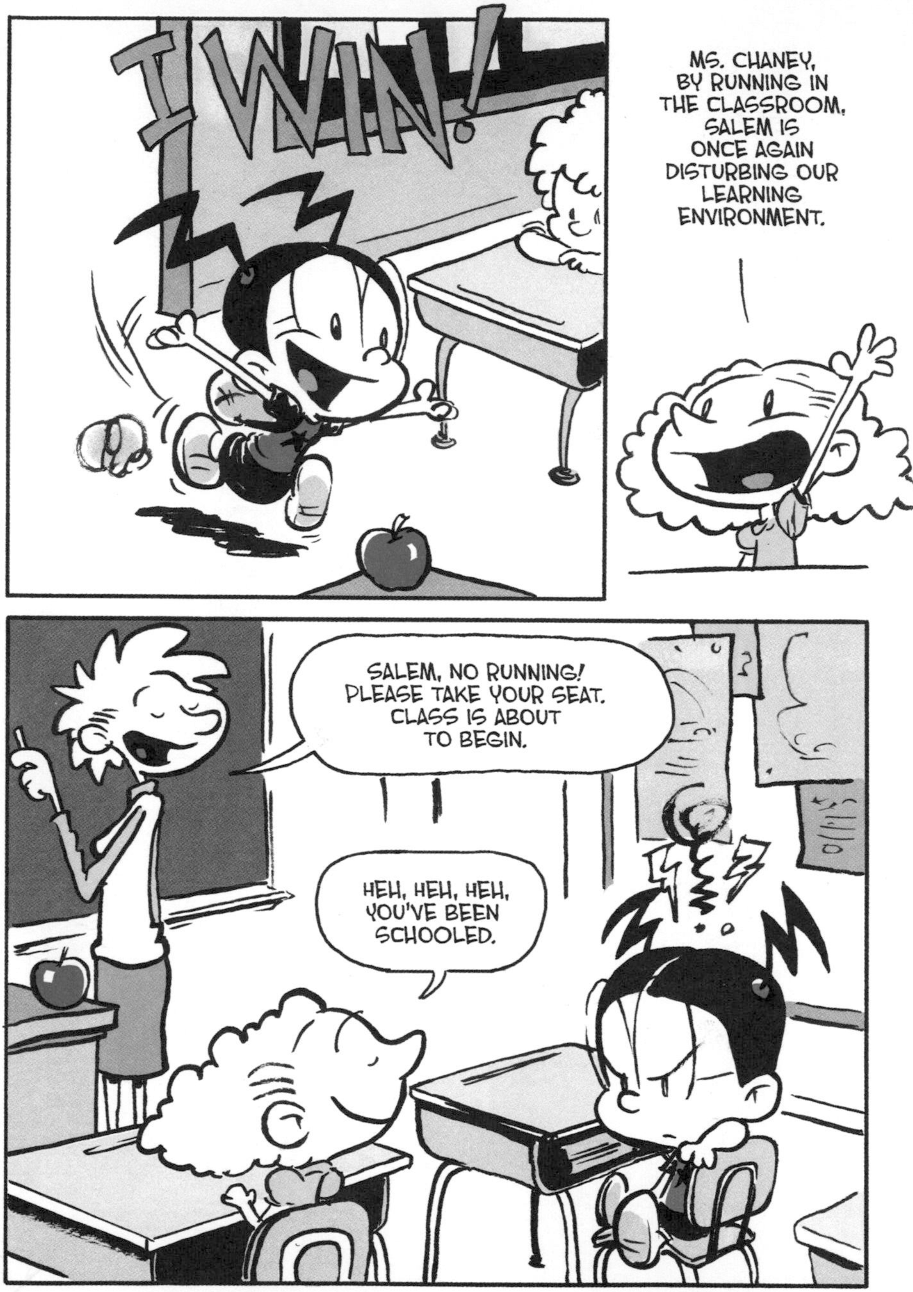
I WIN!
MS. CHANEY, BY RUNNING IN THE CLASSROOM, SALEM IS ONCE AGAIN DISTURBING OUR LEARNING ENVIRONMENT.
SALEM, NO RUNNING! PLEASE TAKE YOUR SEAT. CLASS IS ABOUT TO BEGIN.
HEH, HEH, HEH, YOU'VE BEEN SCHOOLED.

Getting to Know Shelly (AS IF YOU'D WANT TO)

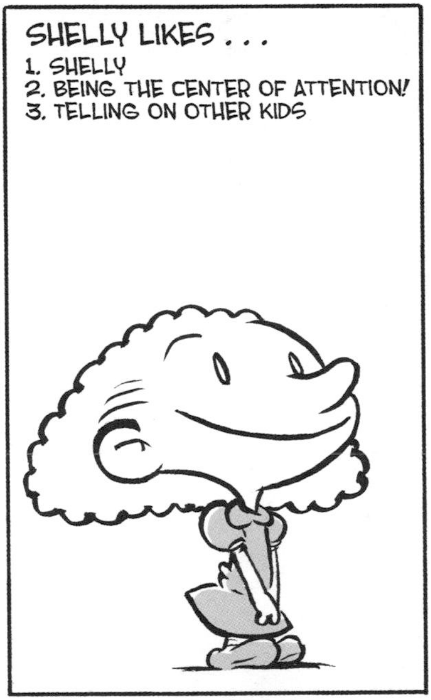
SHELLY LIKES . . .
1. SHELLY
2. BEING THE CENTER OF ATTENTION!
3. TELLING ON OTHER KIDS

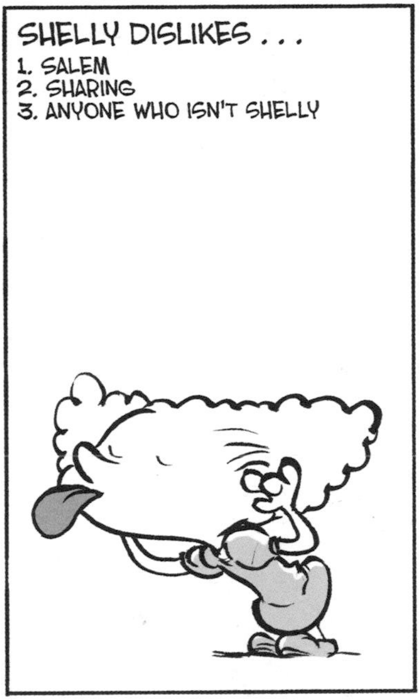
SHELLY DISLIKES . . .
1. SALEM
2. SHARING
3. ANYONE WHO ISN'T SHELLY

POWERS

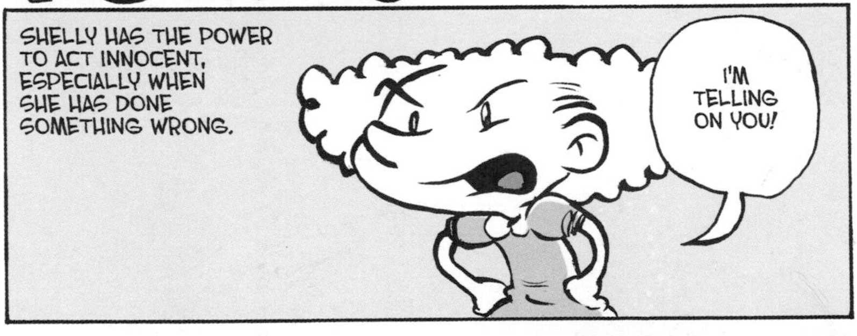
SHELLY HAS THE POWER TO ACT INNOCENT, ESPECIALLY WHEN SHE HAS DONE SOMETHING WRONG.
I'M TELLING ON YOU!

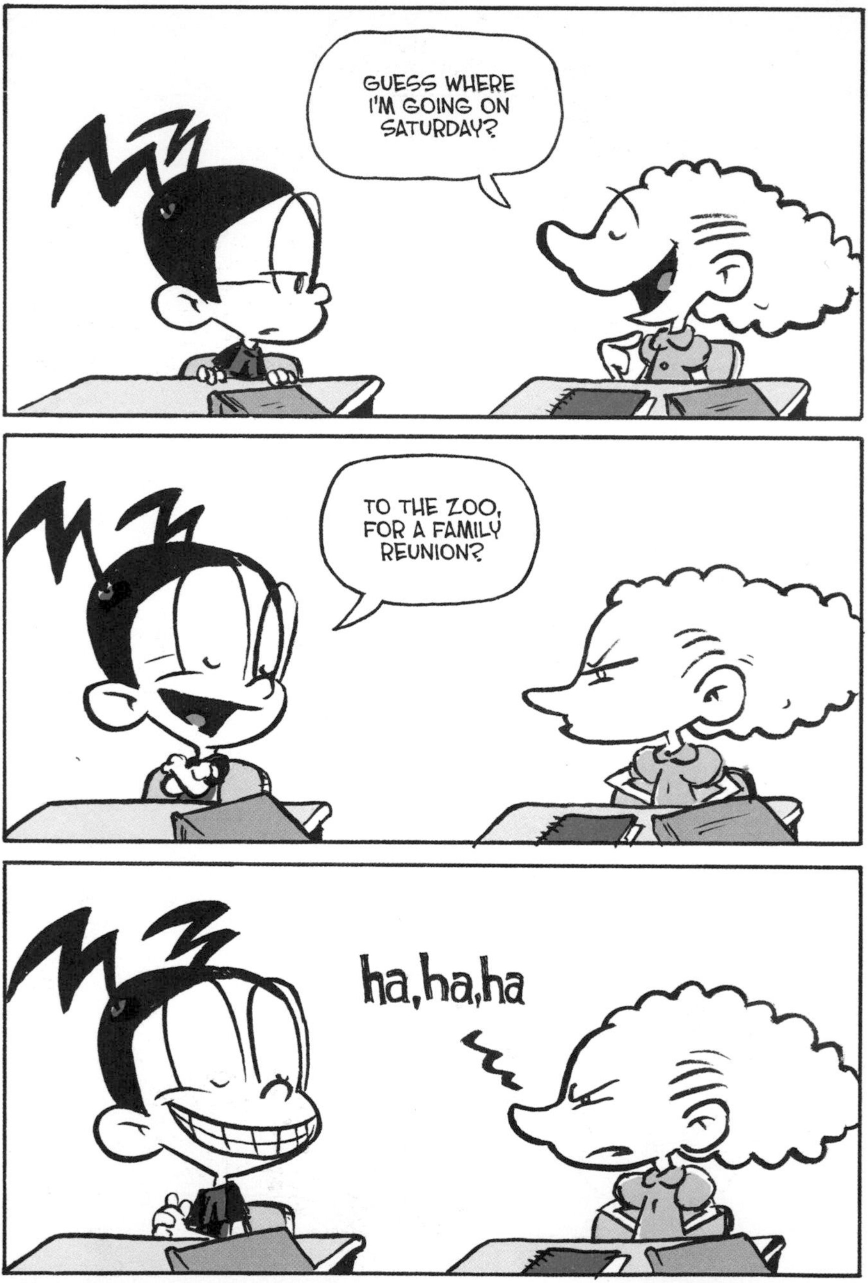
GUESS WHERE I'M GOING ON SATURDAY?
TO THE ZOO, FOR A FAMILY REUNION?
ha,ha,ha

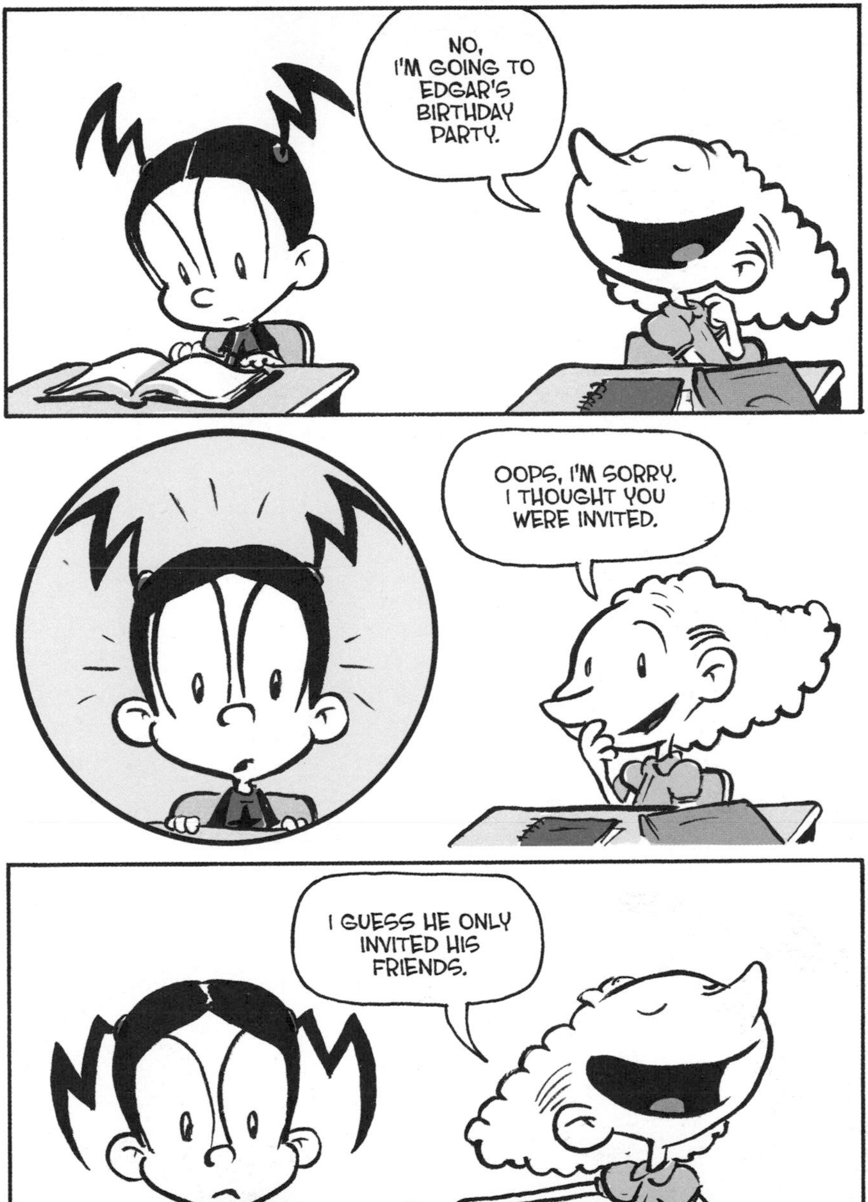

NO, I'M GOING TO EDGAR'S BIRTHDAY PARTY.
OOPS, I'M SORRY. I THOUGHT YOU WERE INVITED.
I GUESS HE ONLY INVITED HIS FRIENDS.

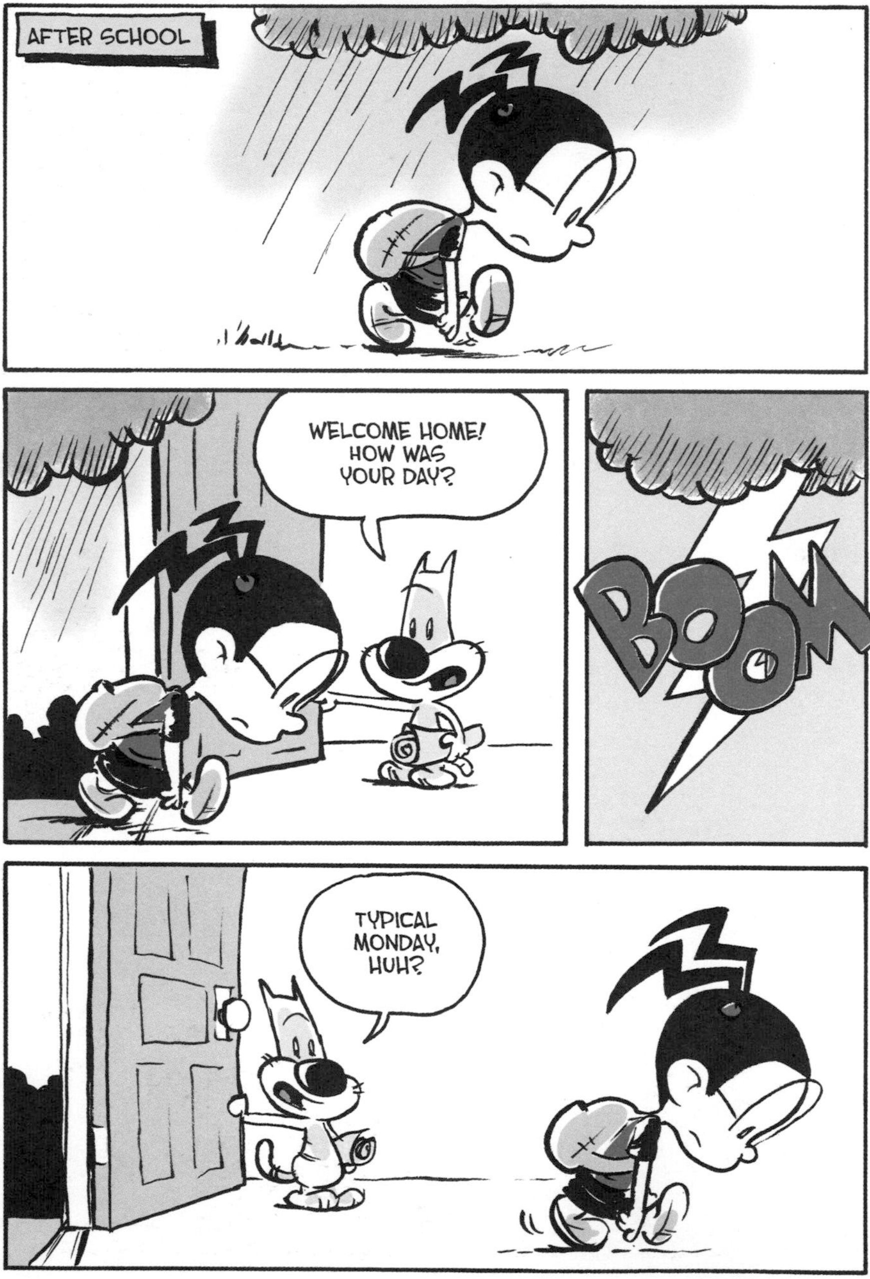
AFTER SCHOOL
WELCOME HOME! HOW WAS YOUR DAY?
BOOM
TYPICAL MONDAY, HUH?

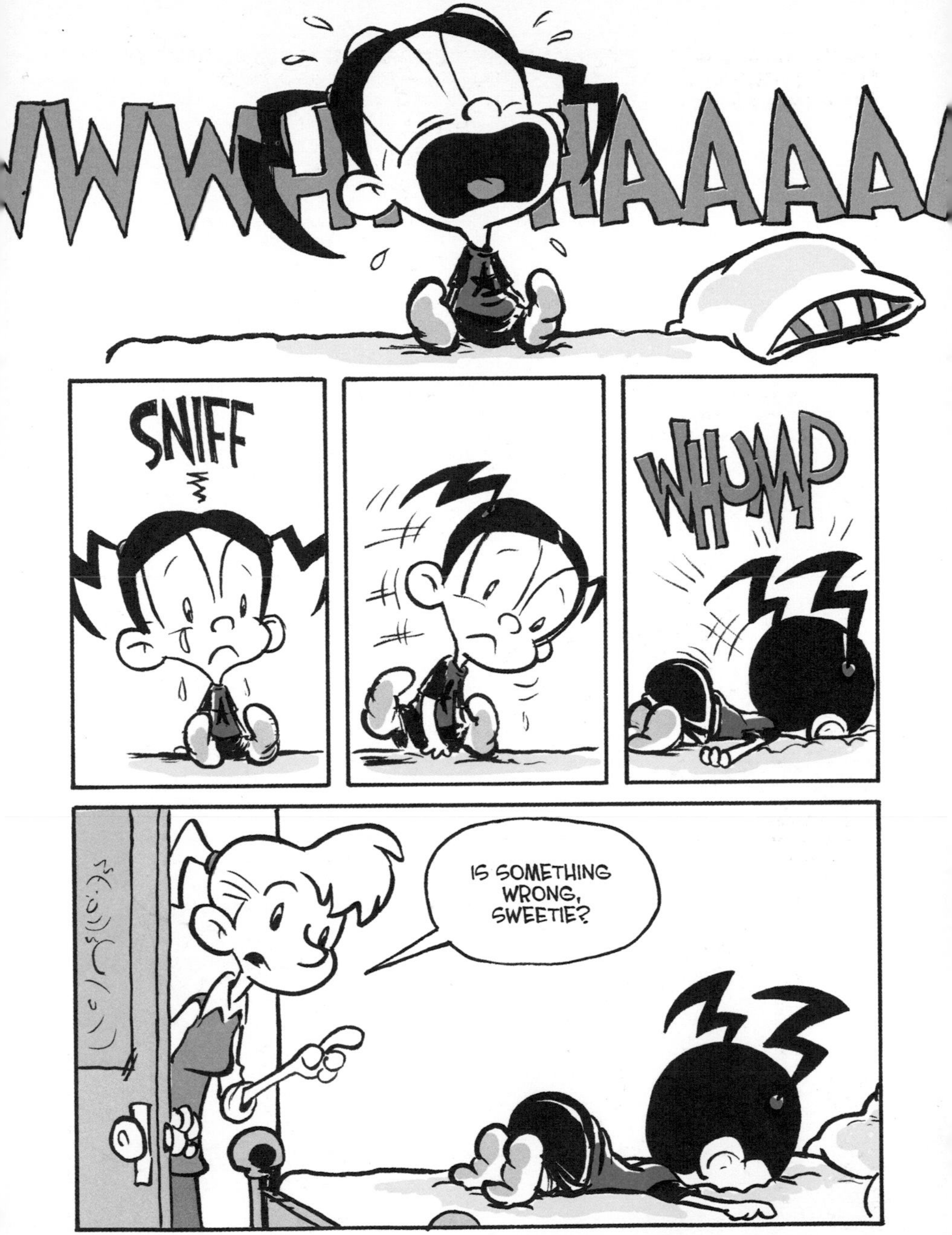
WWWHAAAAAA
SNIFF
WHUMP
IS SOMETHING WRONG, SWEETIE?

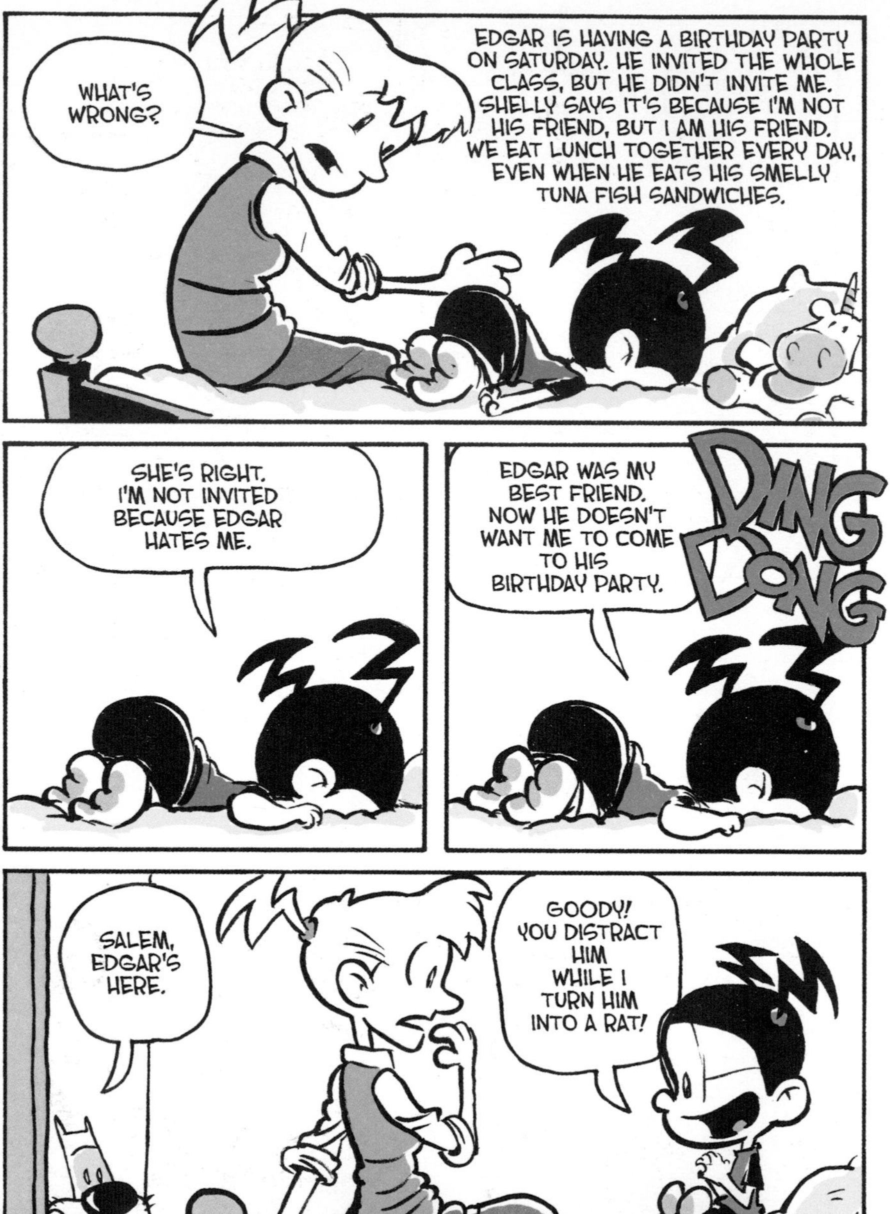
WHAT'S WRONG?
EDGAR IS HAVING A BIRTHDAY PARTY ON SATURDAY. HE INVITED THE WHOLE CLASS, BUT HE DIDN'T INVITE ME. SHELLY SAYS IT'S BECAUSE I'M NOT HIS FRIEND, BUT I AM HIS FRIEND. WE EAT LUNCH TOGETHER EVERY DAY, EVEN WHEN HE EATS HIS SMELLY TUNA FISH SANDWICHES.
SHE'S RIGHT. I'M NOT INVITED BECAUSE EDGAR HATES ME.
EDGAR WAS MY BEST FRIEND. NOW HE DOESN'T WANT ME TO COME TO HIS BIRTHDAY PARTY.
DING DONG
SALEM, EDGAR'S HERE.
GOODY! YOU DISTRACT HIM WHILE I TURN HIM INTO A RAT!

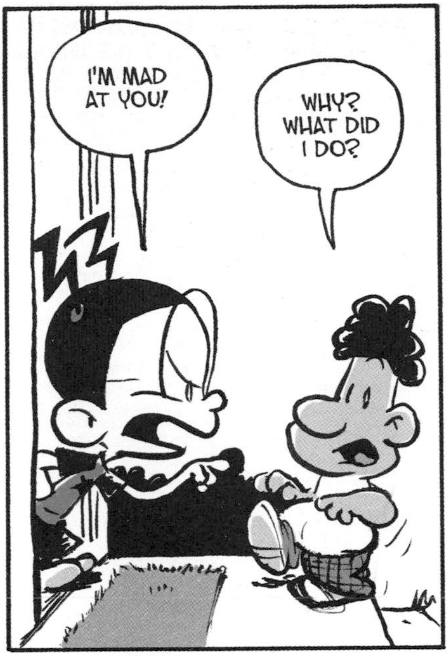
I'M MAD AT YOU!
WHY? WHAT DID I DO?

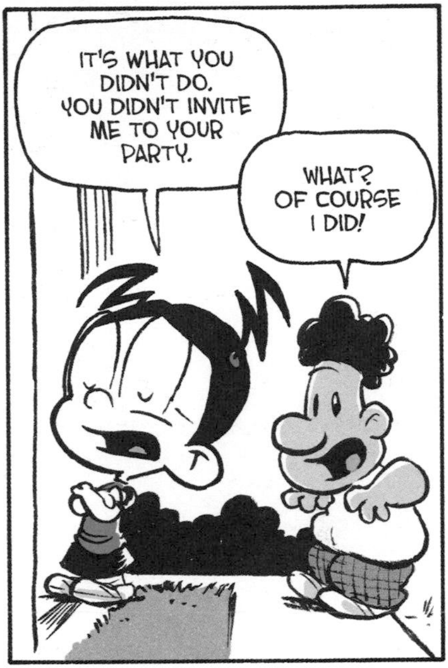
IT'S WHAT YOU DIDN'T DO. YOU DIDN'T INVITE ME TO YOUR PARTY.
WHAT? OF COURSE I DID!

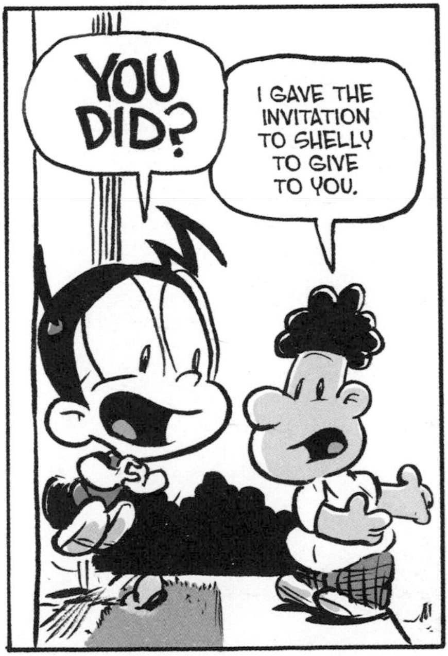
YOU DID?
I GAVE THE INVITATION TO SHELLY TO GIVE TO YOU.

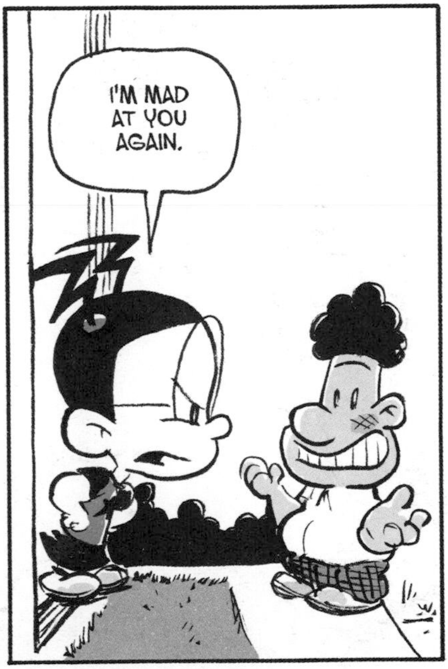
I'M MAD AT YOU AGAIN.

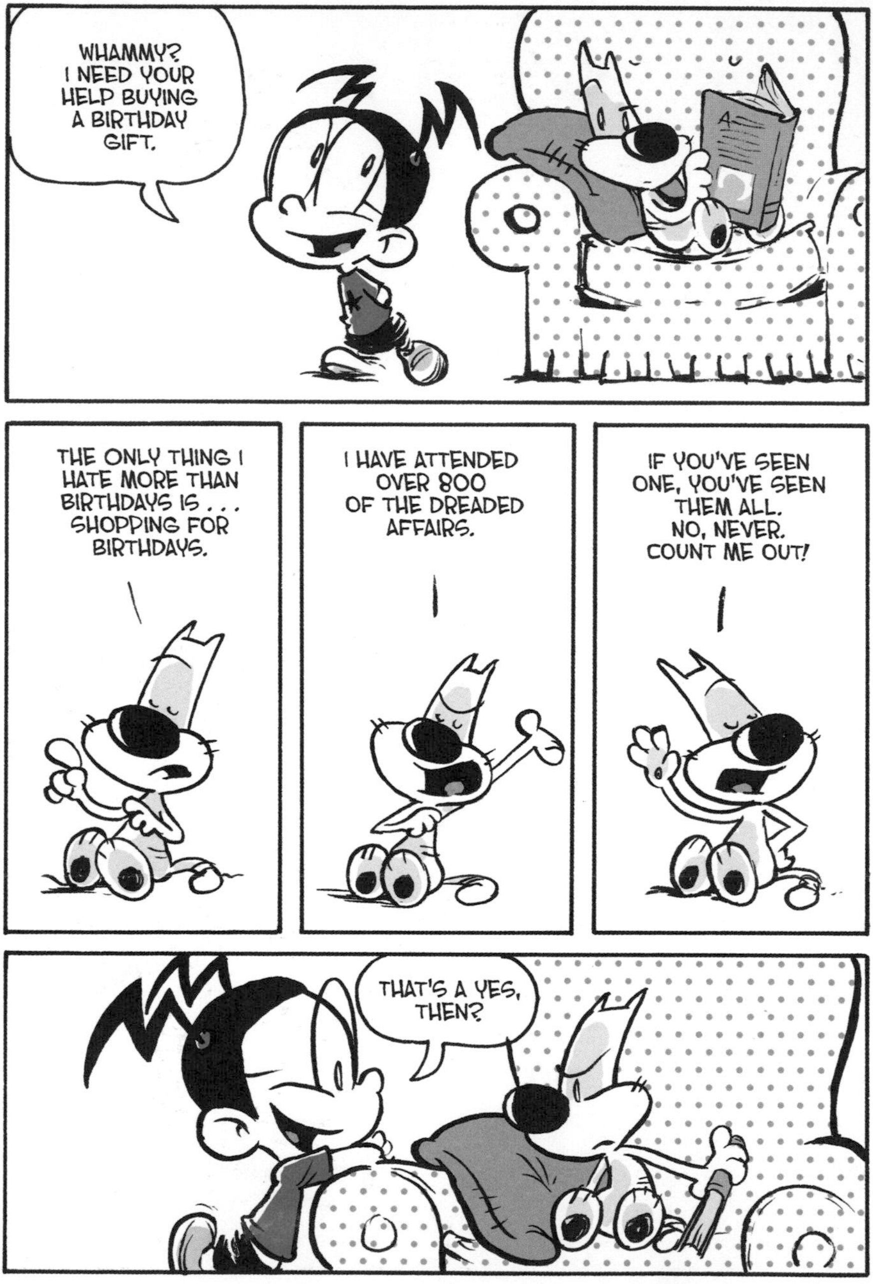
WHAMMY? I NEED YOUR HELP BUYING A BIRTHDAY GIFT.
THE ONLY THING I HATE MORE THAN BIRTHDAYS IS . . . SHOPPING FOR BIRTHDAYS.
I HAVE ATTENDED OVER 800 OF THE DREADED AFFAIRS.
IF YOU'VE SEEN ONE, YOU'VE SEEN THEM ALL. NO, NEVER. COUNT ME OUT!
THAT'S A YES, THEN?

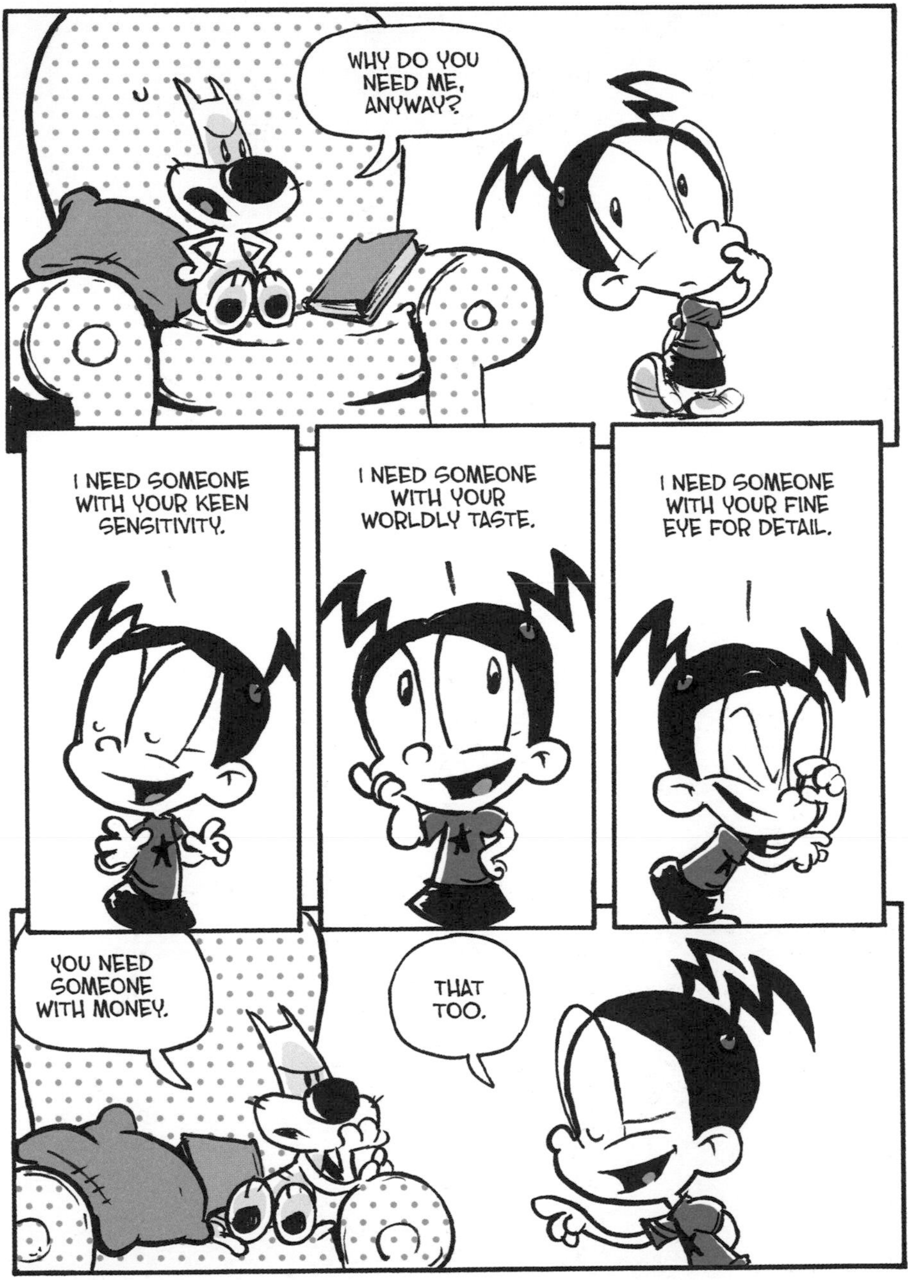
WHY DO YOU NEED ME, ANYWAY?
I NEED SOMEONE WITH YOUR KEEN SENSITIVITY.
I NEED SOMEONE WITH YOUR WORLDLY TASTE.
I NEED SOMEONE WITH YOUR FINE EYE FOR DETAIL.
YOU NEED SOMEONE WITH MONEY.
THAT TOO.

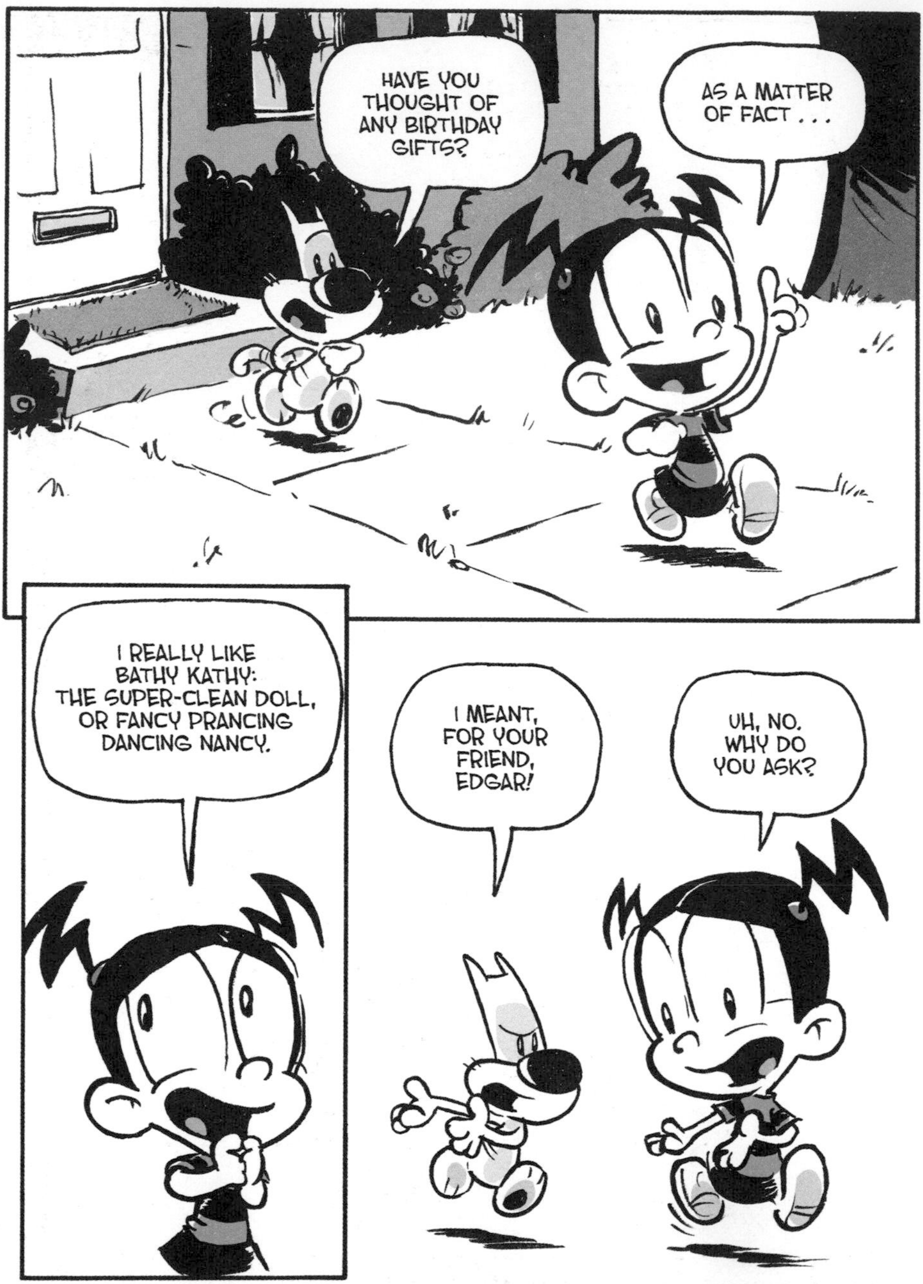
HAVE YOU THOUGHT OF ANY BIRTHDAY GIFTS?
AS A MATTER OF FACT . . .
I REALLY LIKE BATHY KATHY: THE SUPER-CLEAN DOLL, OR FANCY PRANCING DANCING NANCY.
I MEANT, FOR YOUR FRIEND, EDGAR!
UH, NO. WHY DO YOU ASK?

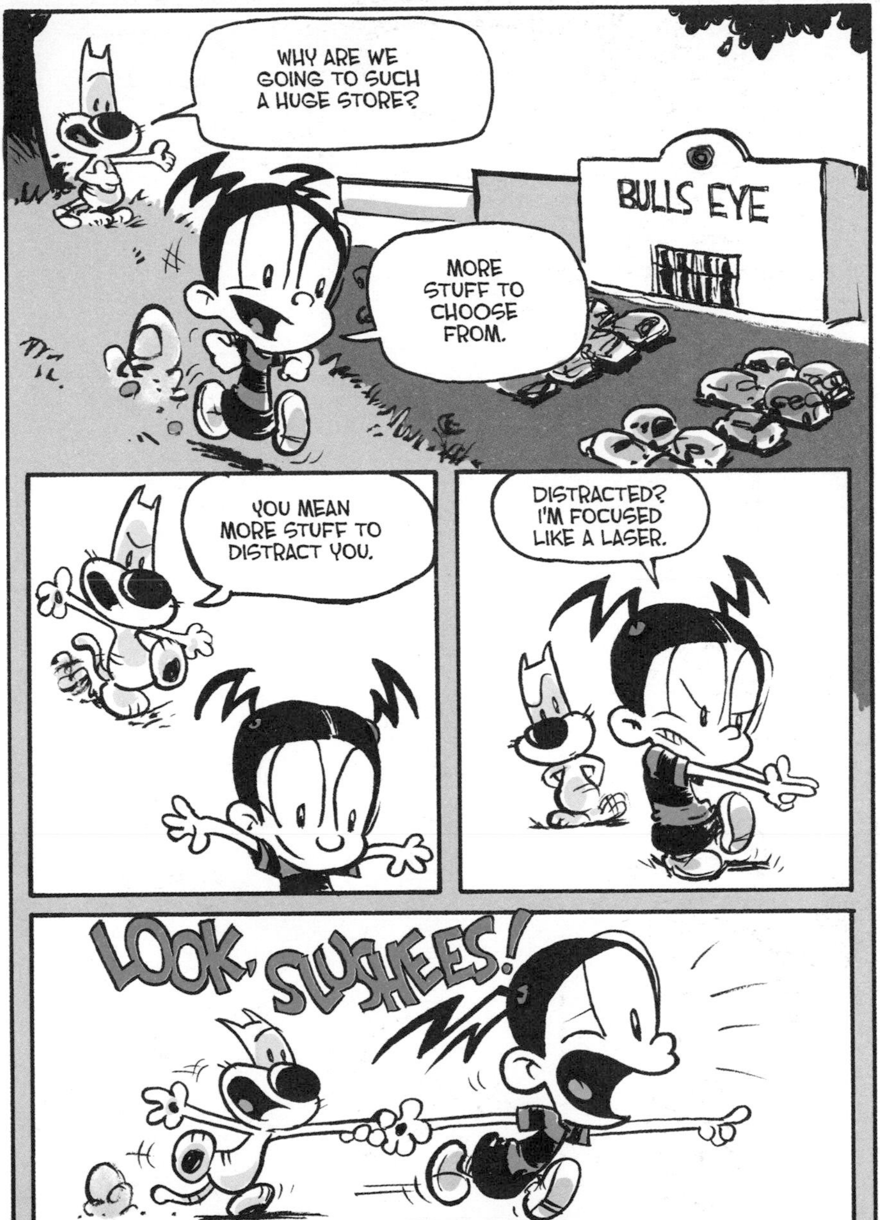
WHY ARE WE GOING TO SUCH A HUGE STORE?
BULLS EYE
MORE STUFF TO CHOOSE FROM.
YOU MEAN MORE STUFF TO DISTRACT YOU.
DISTRACTED? I'M FOCUSED LIKE A LASER.
LOOK, SLUSHEES!

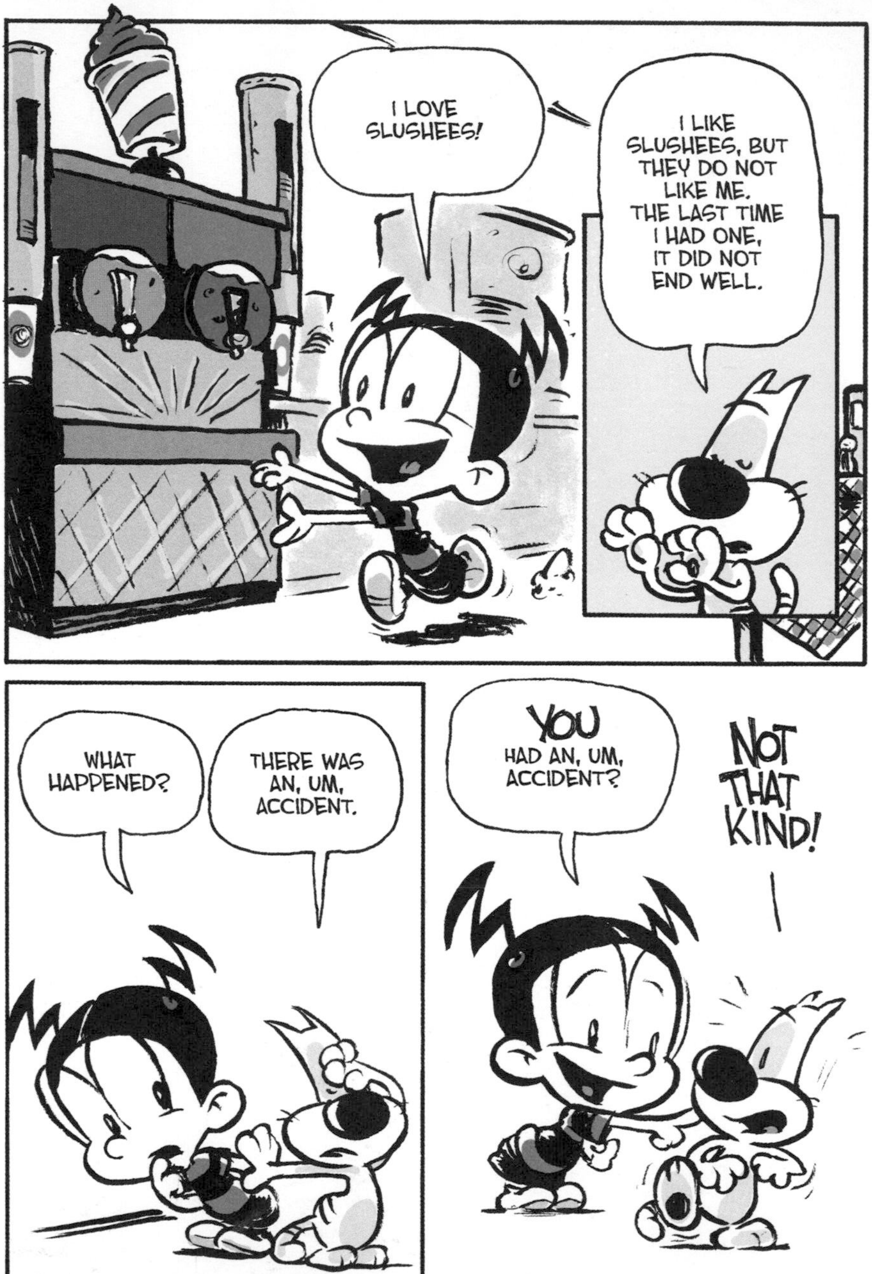
I LOVE SLUSHEES!
I LIKE SLUSHEES, BUT THEY DO NOT LIKE ME. THE LAST TIME I HAD ONE, IT DID NOT END WELL.
WHAT HAPPENED?
THERE WAS AN, UM, ACCIDENT.
YOU HAD AN, UM, ACCIDENT?
NOT THAT KIND!

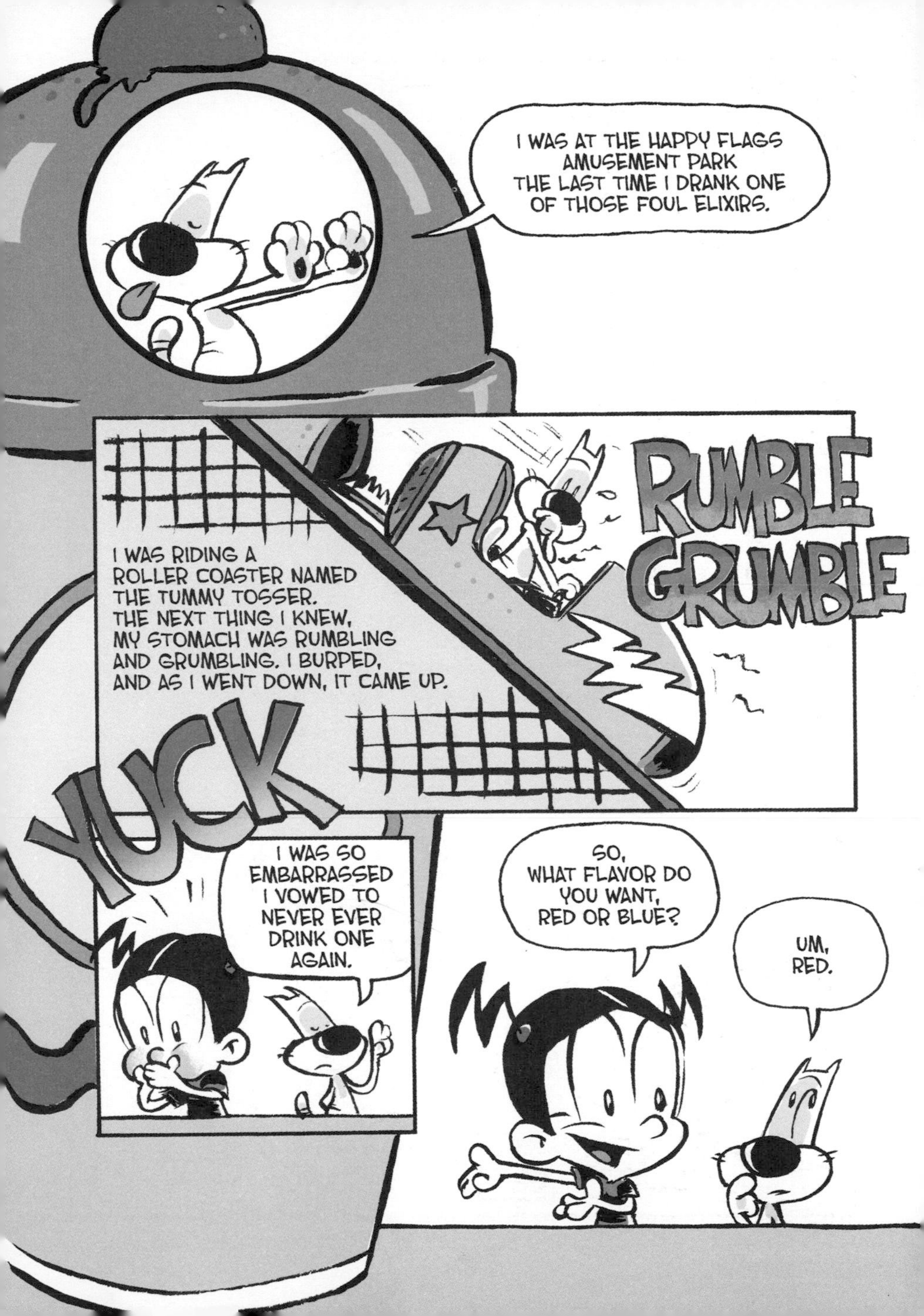
I WAS AT THE HAPPY FLAGS AMUSEMENT PARK THE LAST TIME I DRANK ONE OF THOSE FOUL ELIXIRS.
I WAS RIDING A ROLLER COASTER NAMED THE TUMMY TOSSER. THE NEXT THING I KNEW, MY STOMACH WAS RUMBLING AND GRUMBLING. I BURPED, AND AS I WENT DOWN, IT CAME UP.
RUMBLE GRUMBLE
YUCK
I WAS SO EMBARRASSED I VOWED TO NEVER EVER DRINK ONE AGAIN.
SO, WHAT FLAVOR DO YOU WANT, RED OR BLUE?
UM, RED.

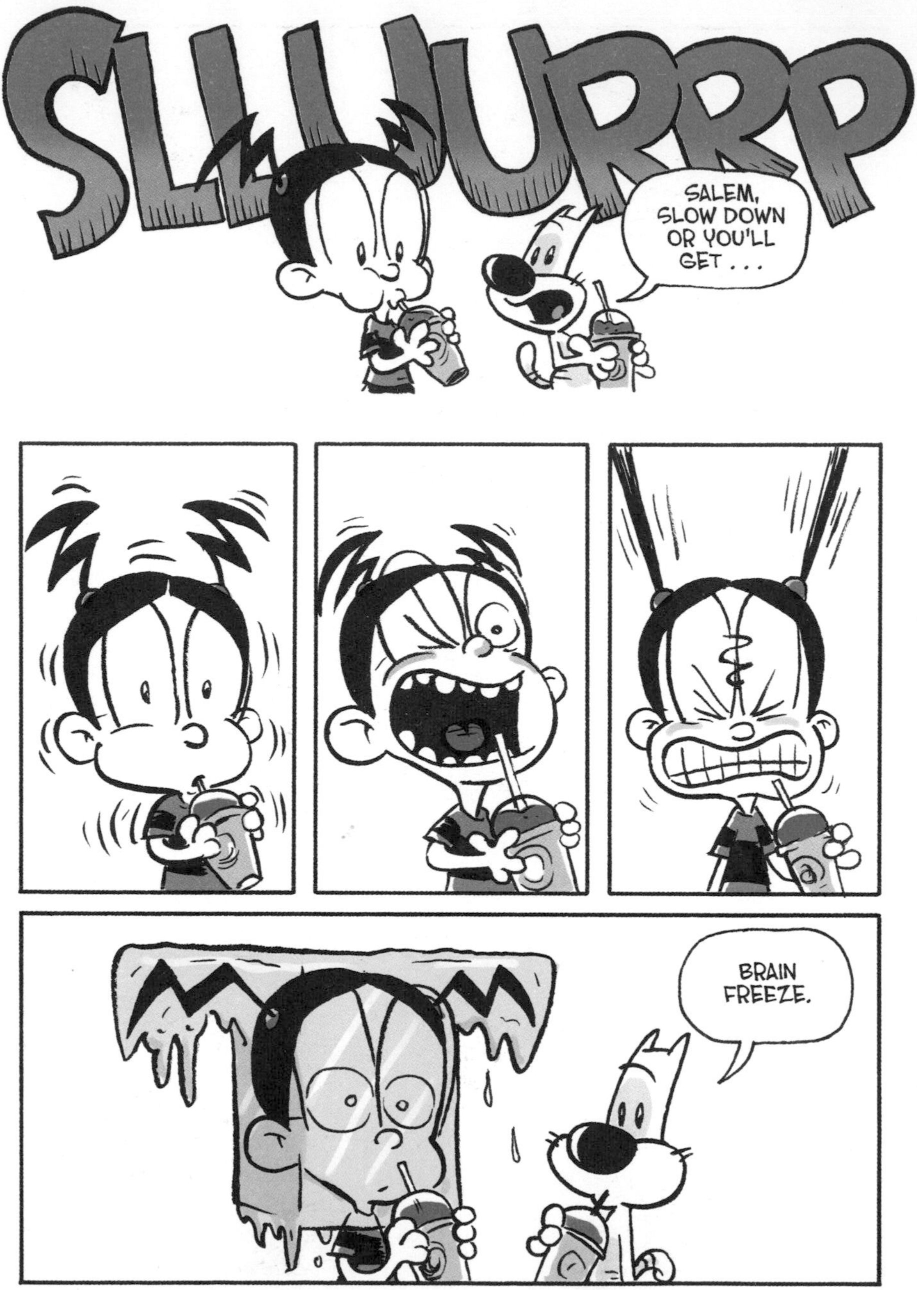
SLLUURRP
SALEM, SLOW DOWN OR YOU'LL GET . . .
BRAIN FREEZE.

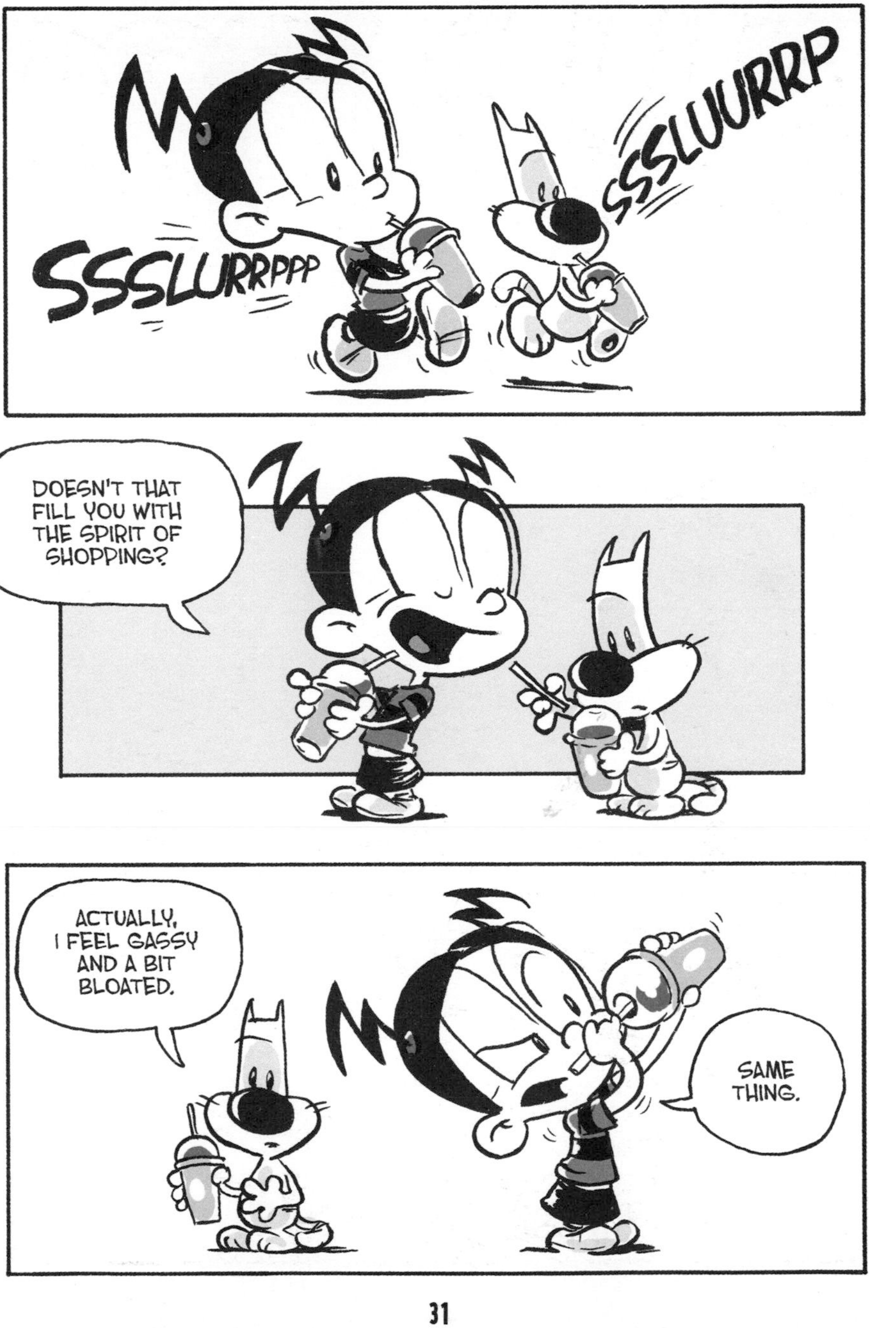
SSSLURRPPP
SSSLUURRP
DOESN'T THAT FILL YOU WITH THE SPIRIT OF SHOPPING?
ACTUALLY, I FEEL GASSY AND A BIT BLOATED.
SAME THING.

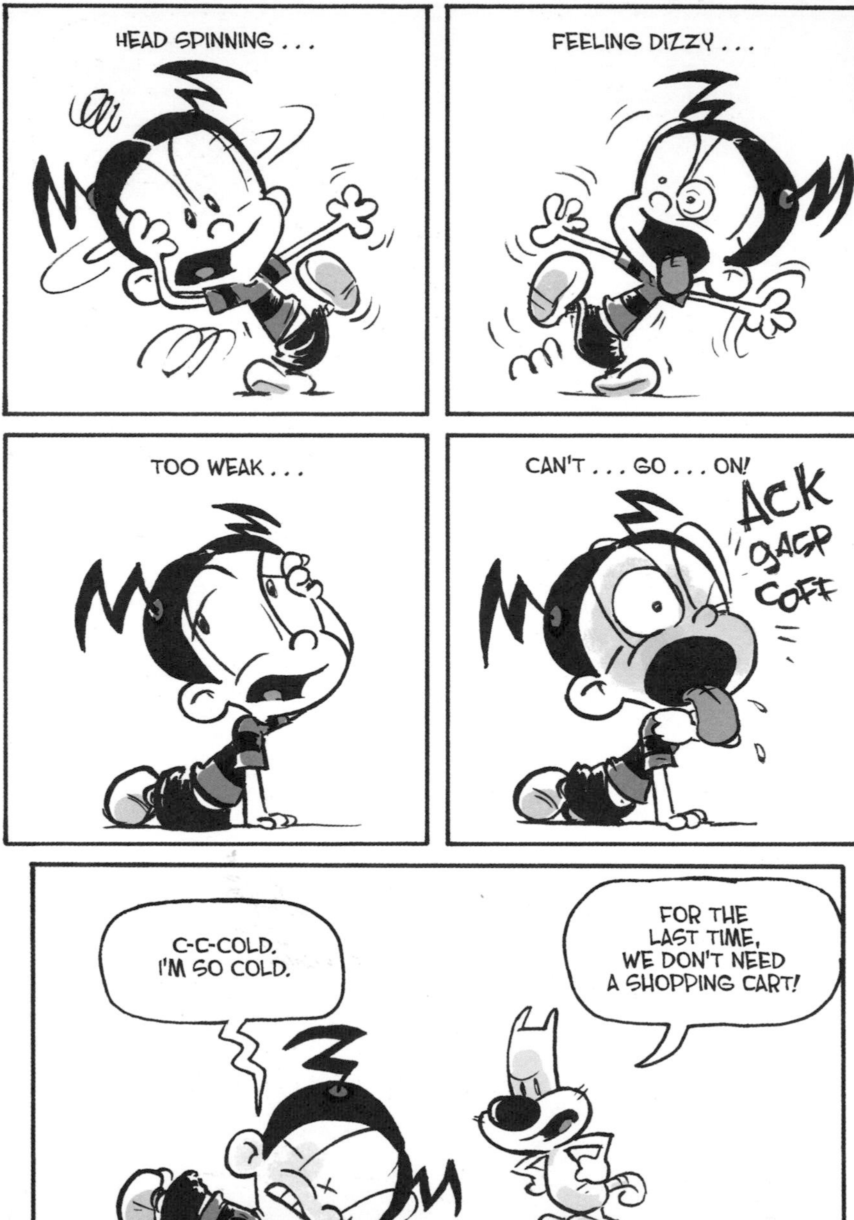
HEAD SPINNING . . .
FEELING DIZZY . . .
TOO WEAK . . .
CAN'T . . . GO . . . ON!
ACK
GASP
COFF
C-C-COLD. I'M SO COLD.
FOR THE LAST TIME, WE DON'T NEED A SHOPPING CART!

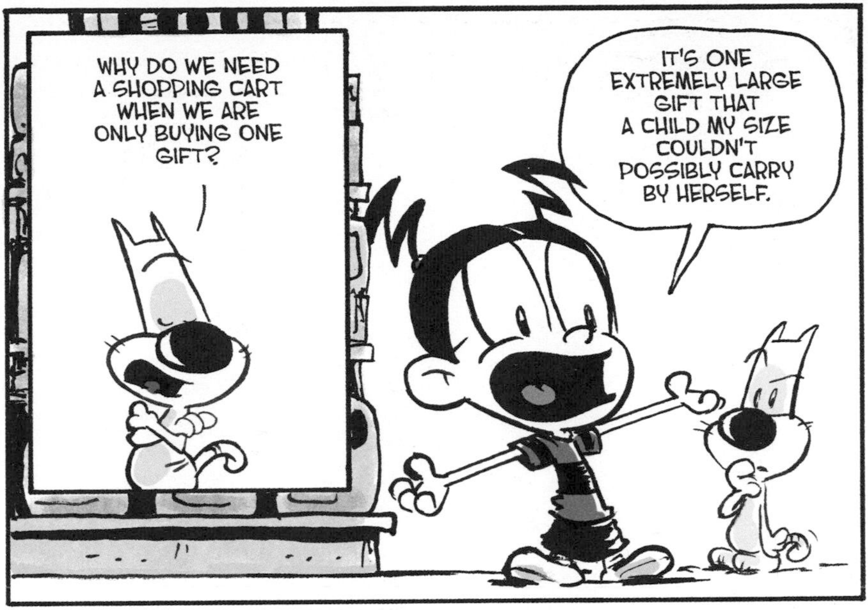
WHY DO WE NEED A SHOPPING CART WHEN WE ARE ONLY BUYING ONE GIFT?
IT'S ONE EXTREMELY LARGE GIFT THAT A CHILD MY SIZE COULDN'T POSSIBLY CARRY BY HERSELF.

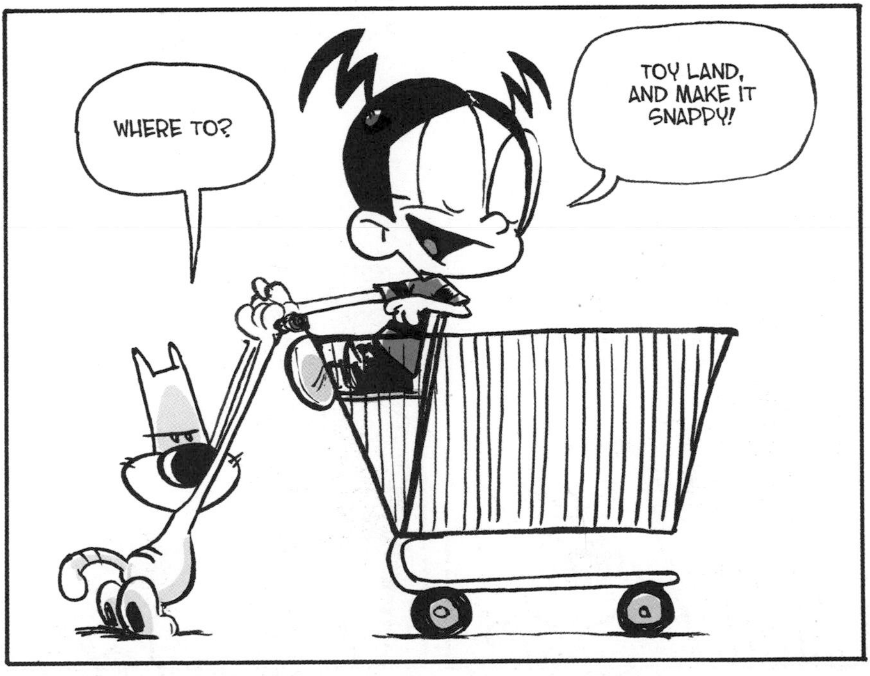
WHERE TO?
TOY LAND, AND MAKE IT SNAPPY!

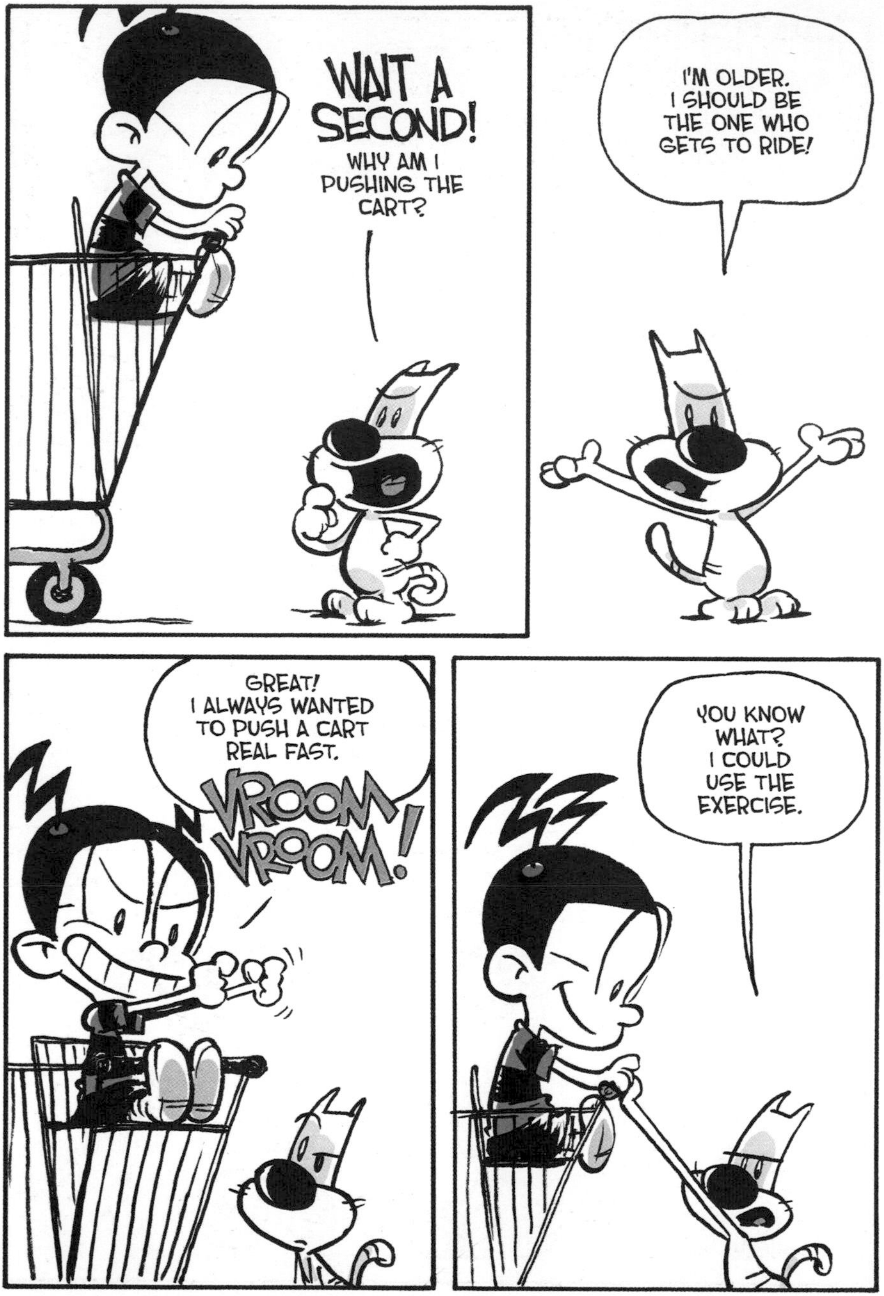
WAIT A SECOND!
WHY AM I PUSHING THE CART?
I'M OLDER. I SHOULD BE THE ONE WHO GETS TO RIDE!
GREAT! I ALWAYS WANTED TO PUSH A CART REAL FAST.
VROOM VROOM!
YOU KNOW WHAT? I COULD USE THE EXERCISE.

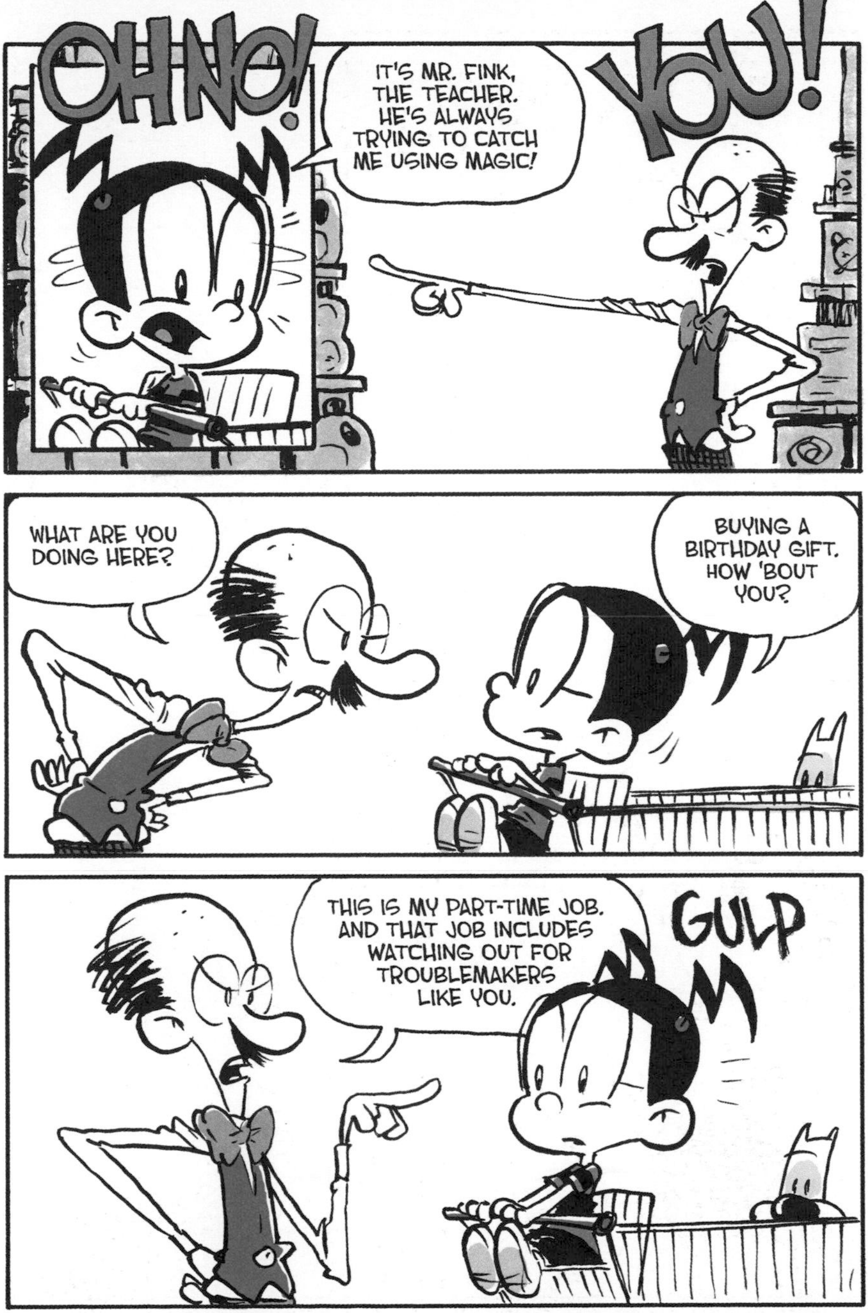
OH NO!
IT'S MR. FINK, THE TEACHER. HE'S ALWAYS TRYING TO CATCH ME USING MAGIC!
YOU!
WHAT ARE YOU DOING HERE?
BUYING A BIRTHDAY GIFT. HOW 'BOUT YOU?
THIS IS MY PART-TIME JOB. AND THAT JOB INCLUDES WATCHING OUT FOR TROUBLEMAKERS LIKE YOU.
GULP

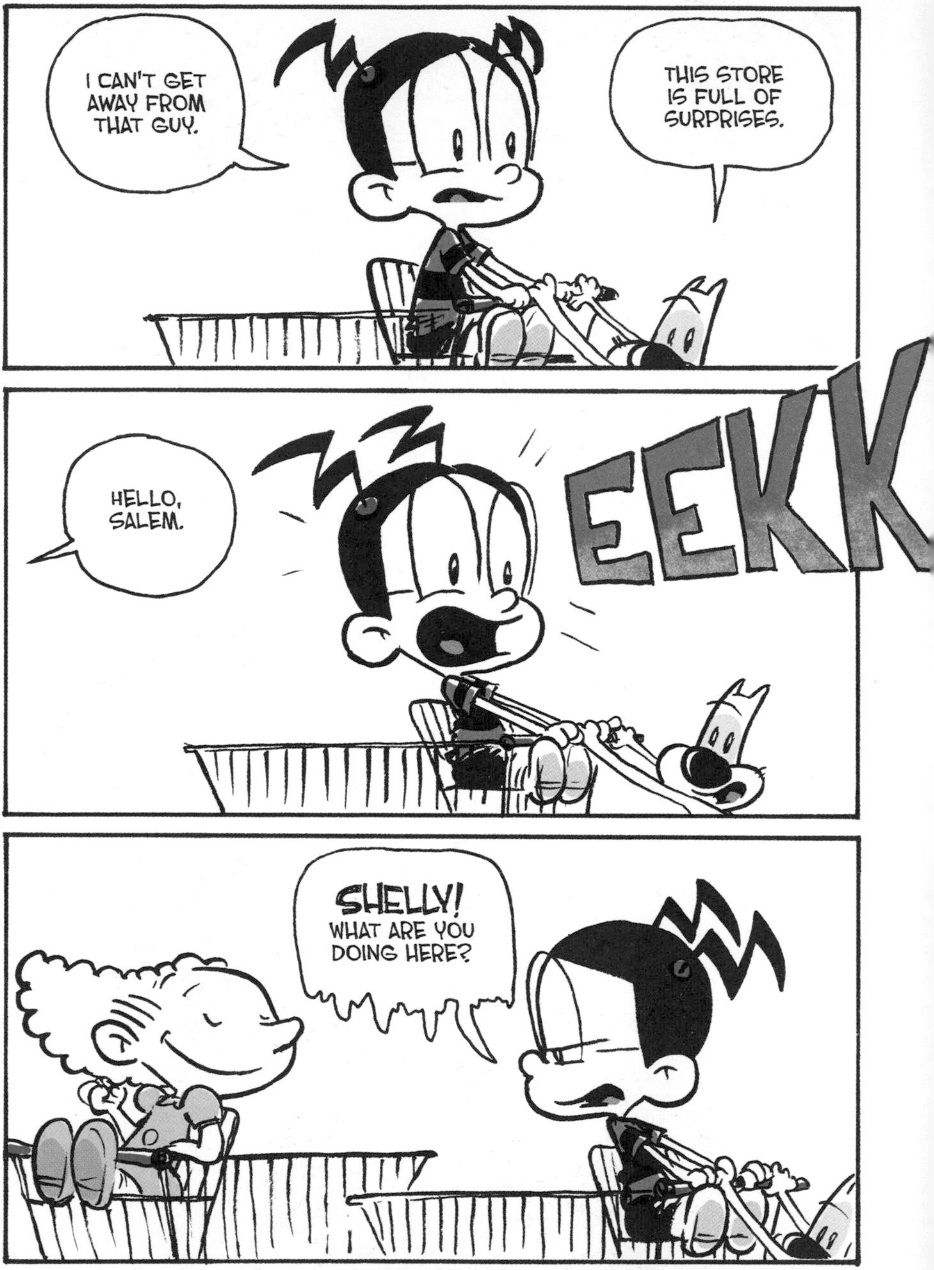
I CAN'T GET AWAY FROM THAT GUY.
THIS STORE IS FULL OF SURPRISES.
HELLO, SALEM.
EEKK
SHELLY! WHAT ARE YOU DOING HERE?

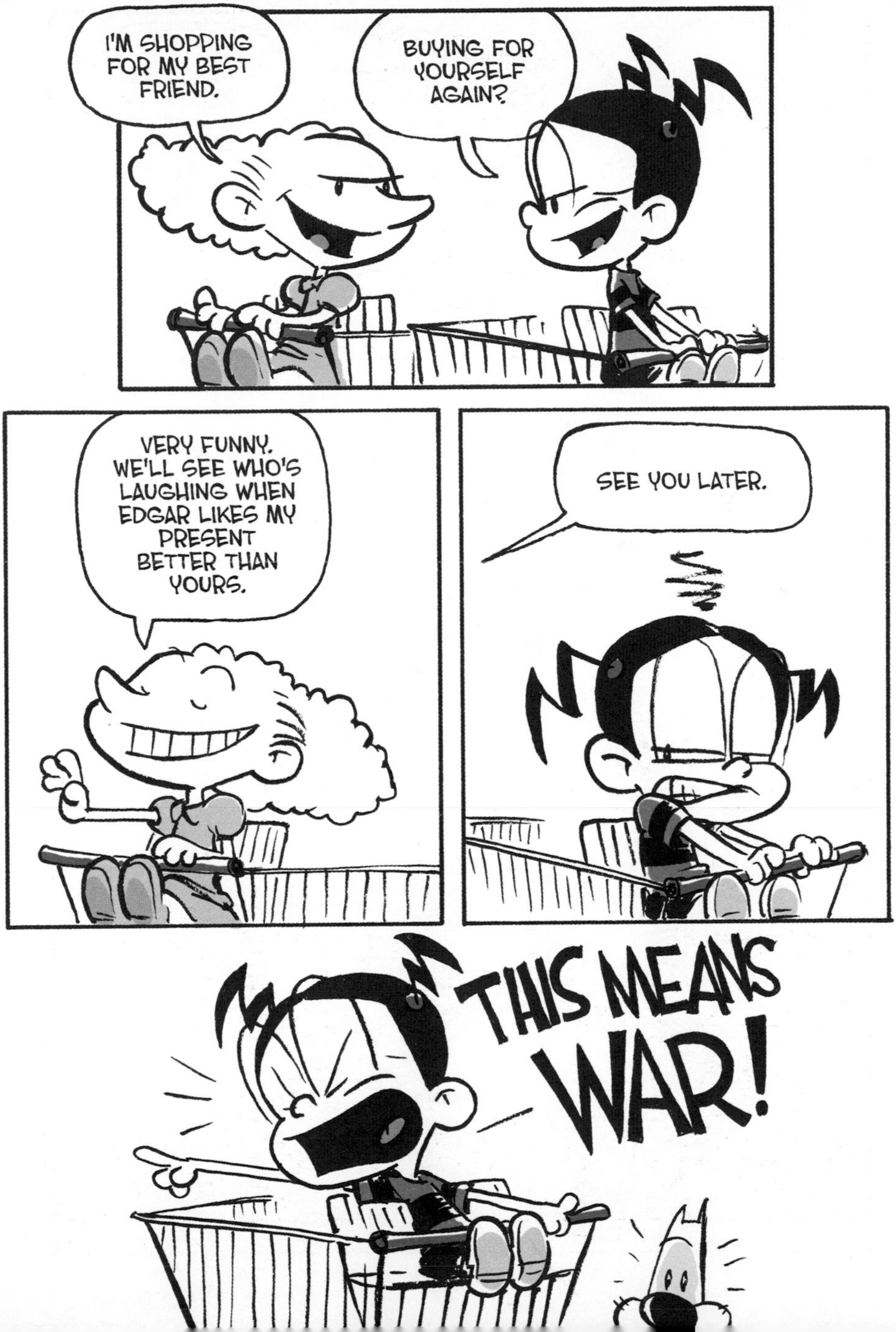
I'M SHOPPING FOR MY BEST FRIEND.
BUYING FOR YOURSELF AGAIN?
VERY FUNNY. WE'LL SEE WHO'S LAUGHING WHEN EDGAR LIKES MY PRESENT BETTER THAN YOURS.
SEE YOU LATER.
THIS MEANS WAR!

41

46

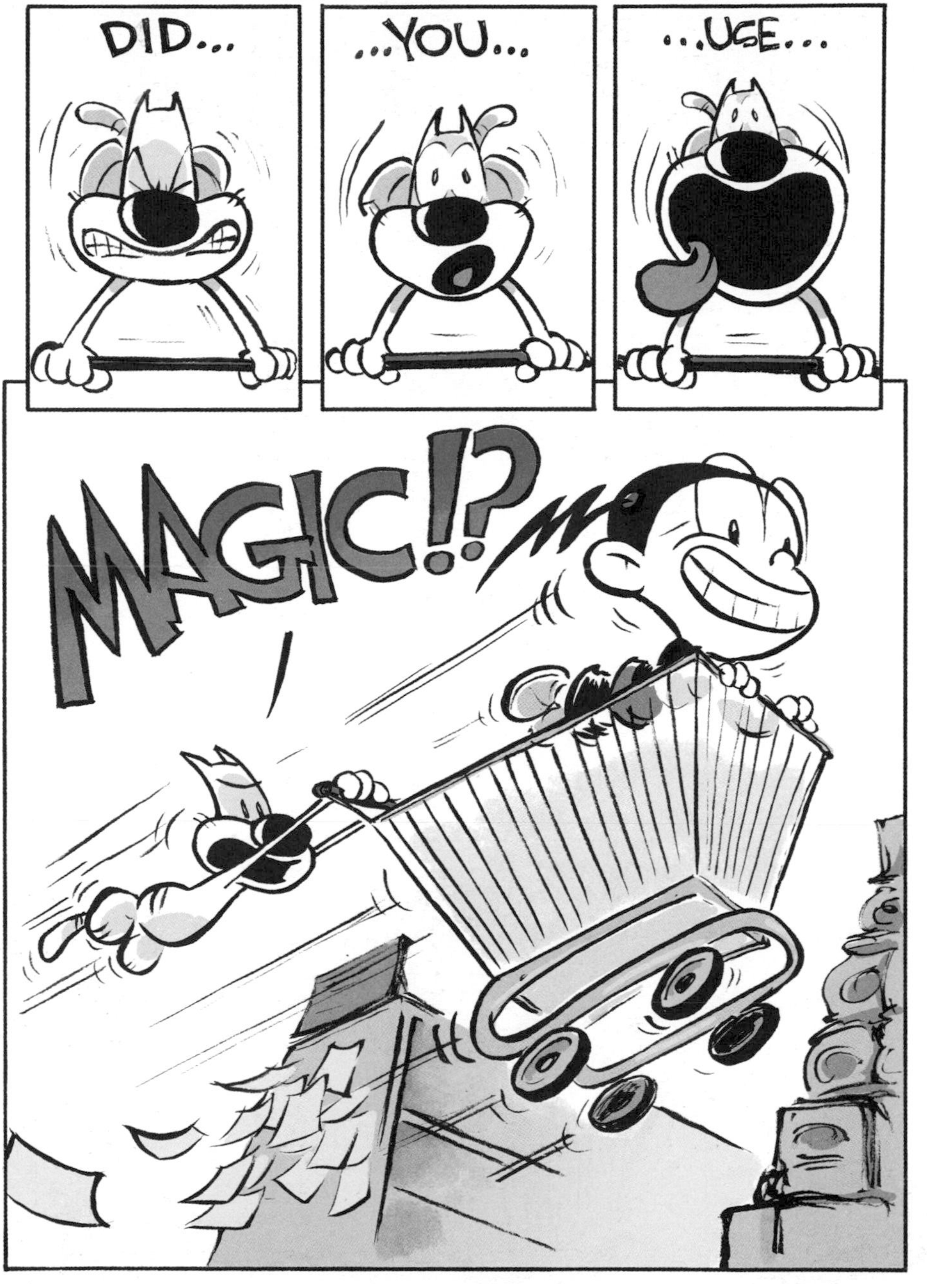
DID...
...YOU...
...USE...
MAGIC!?

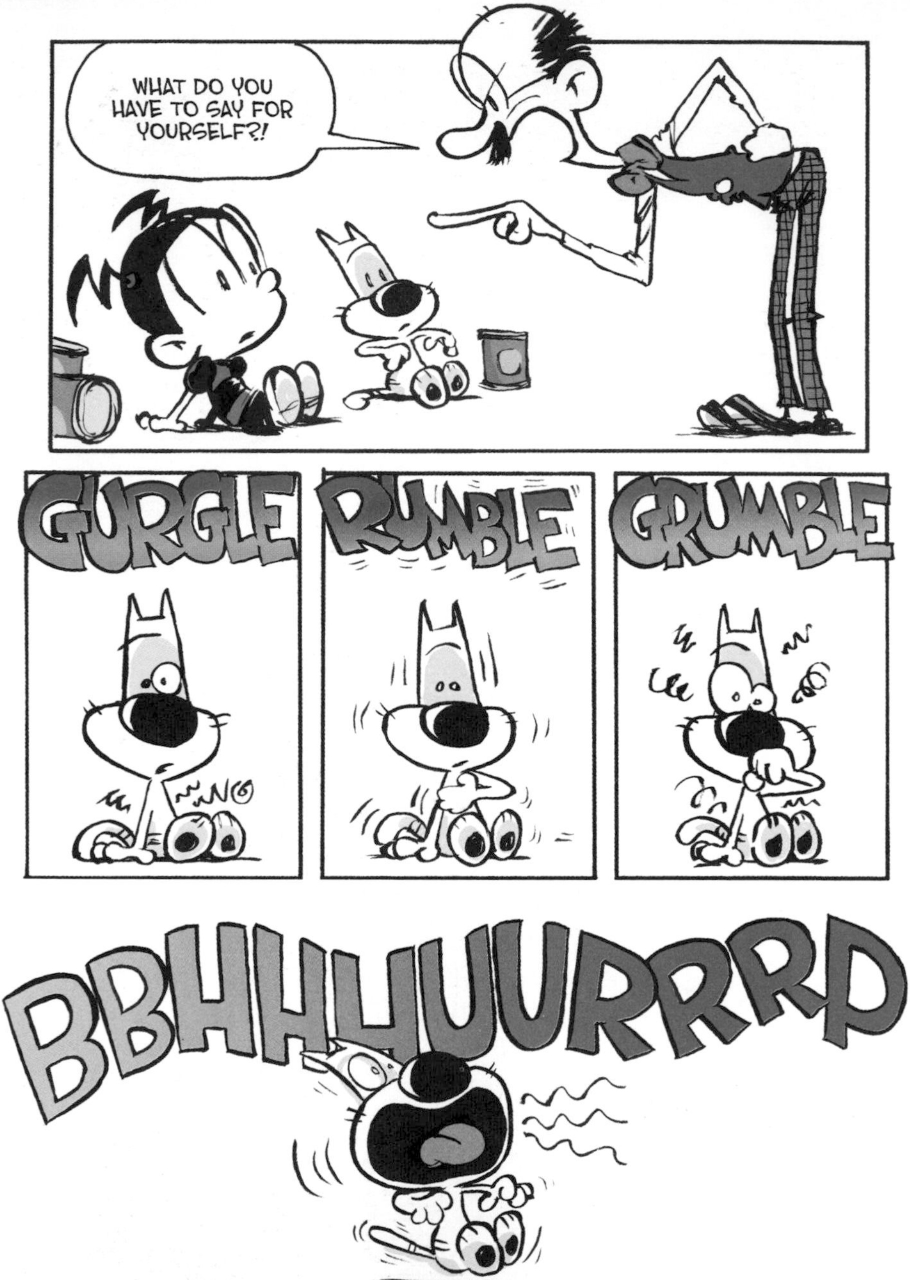
WHAT DO YOU HAVE TO SAY FOR YOURSELF?!
GURGLE
RUMBLE
GRUMBLE
BBHHUURRRD

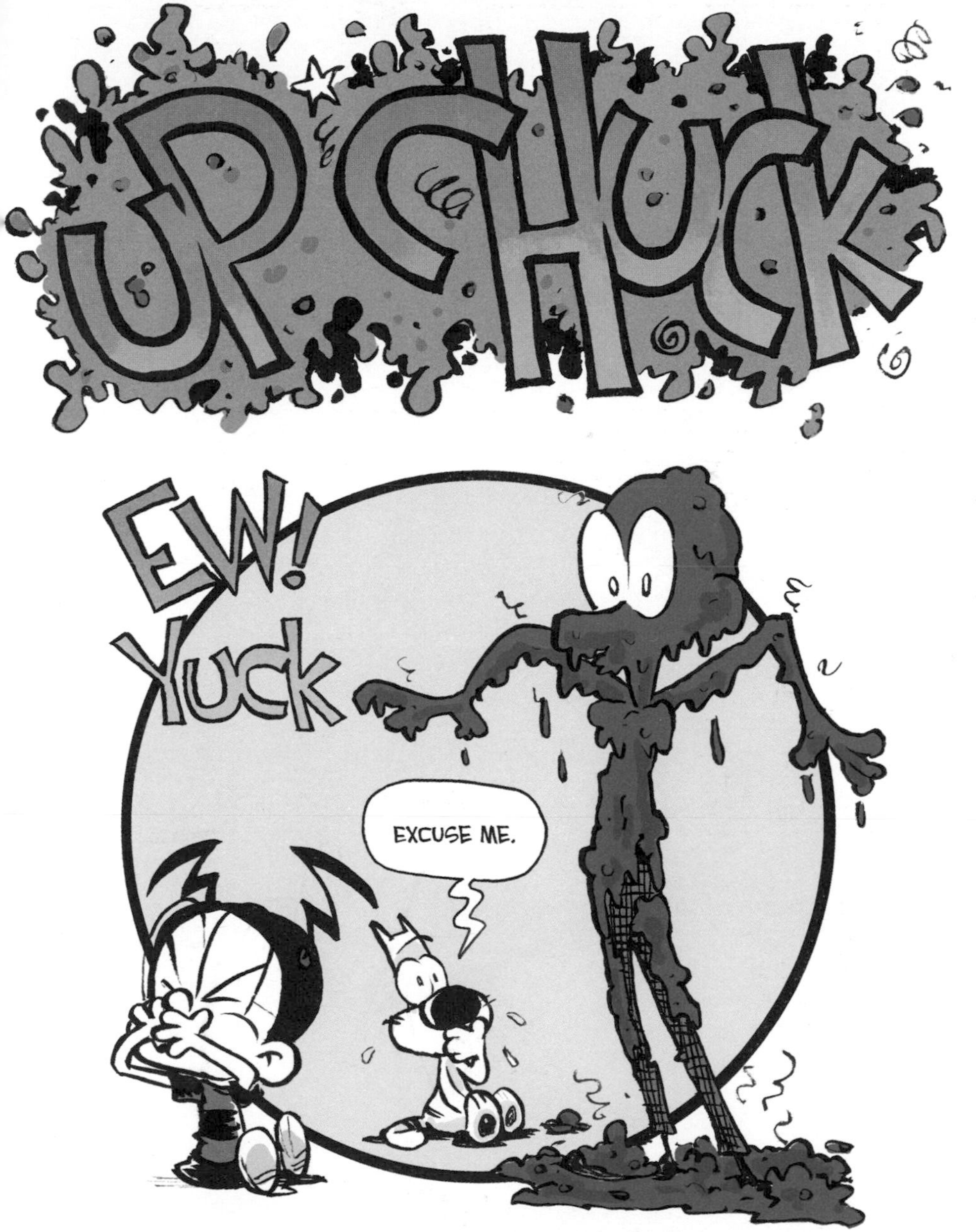
UP CHUCK
EW!
YUCK
EXCUSE ME.

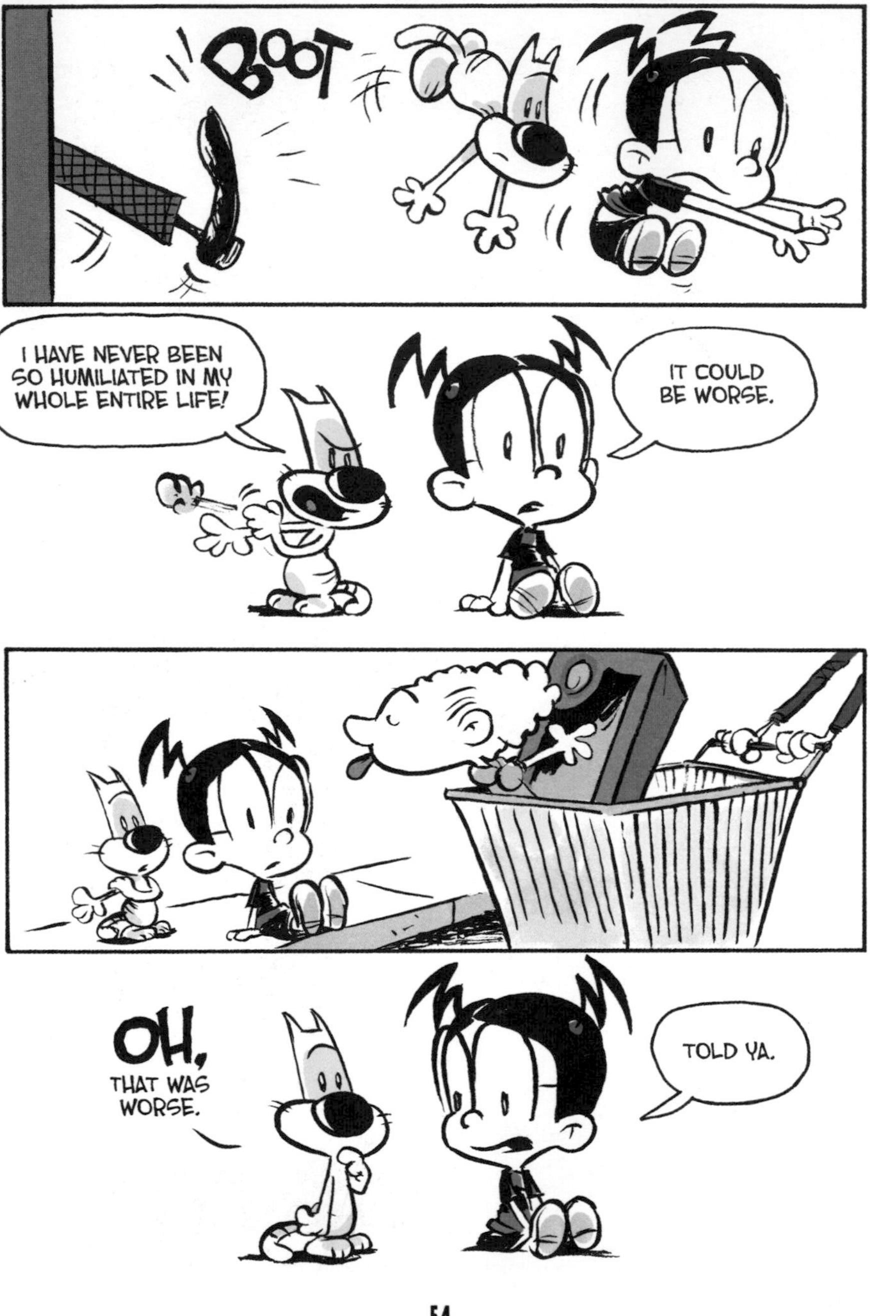
BOOT
I HAVE NEVER BEEN SO HUMILIATED IN MY WHOLE ENTIRE LIFE!
IT COULD BE WORSE.
OH, THAT WAS WORSE.
TOLD YA.

55

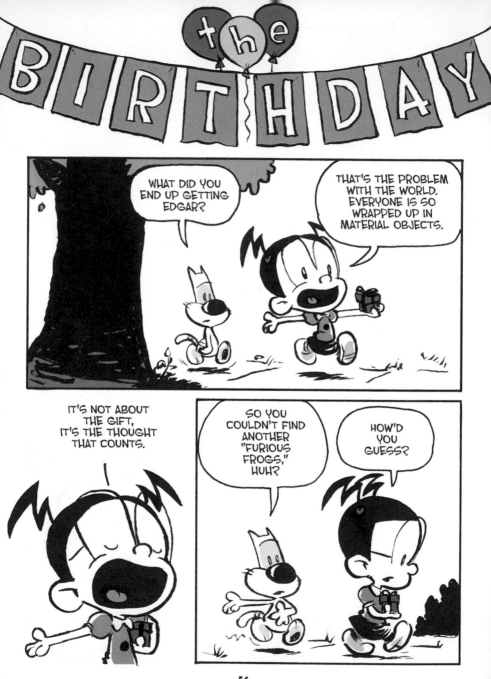

57

58

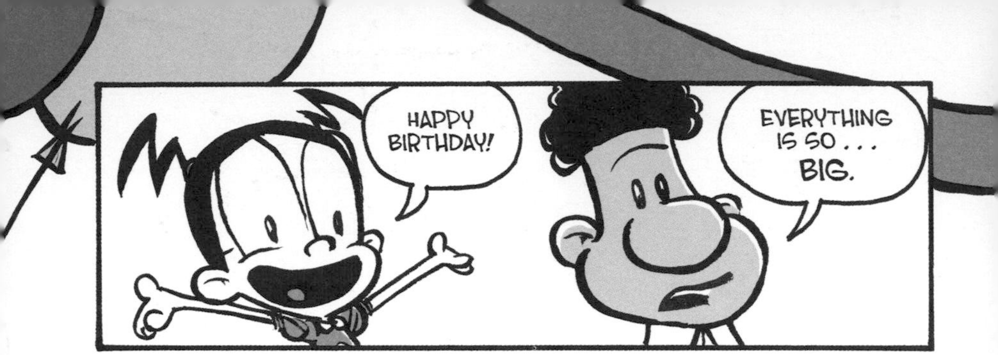
HAPPY BIRTHDAY!
EVERYTHING IS SO . . . BIG.
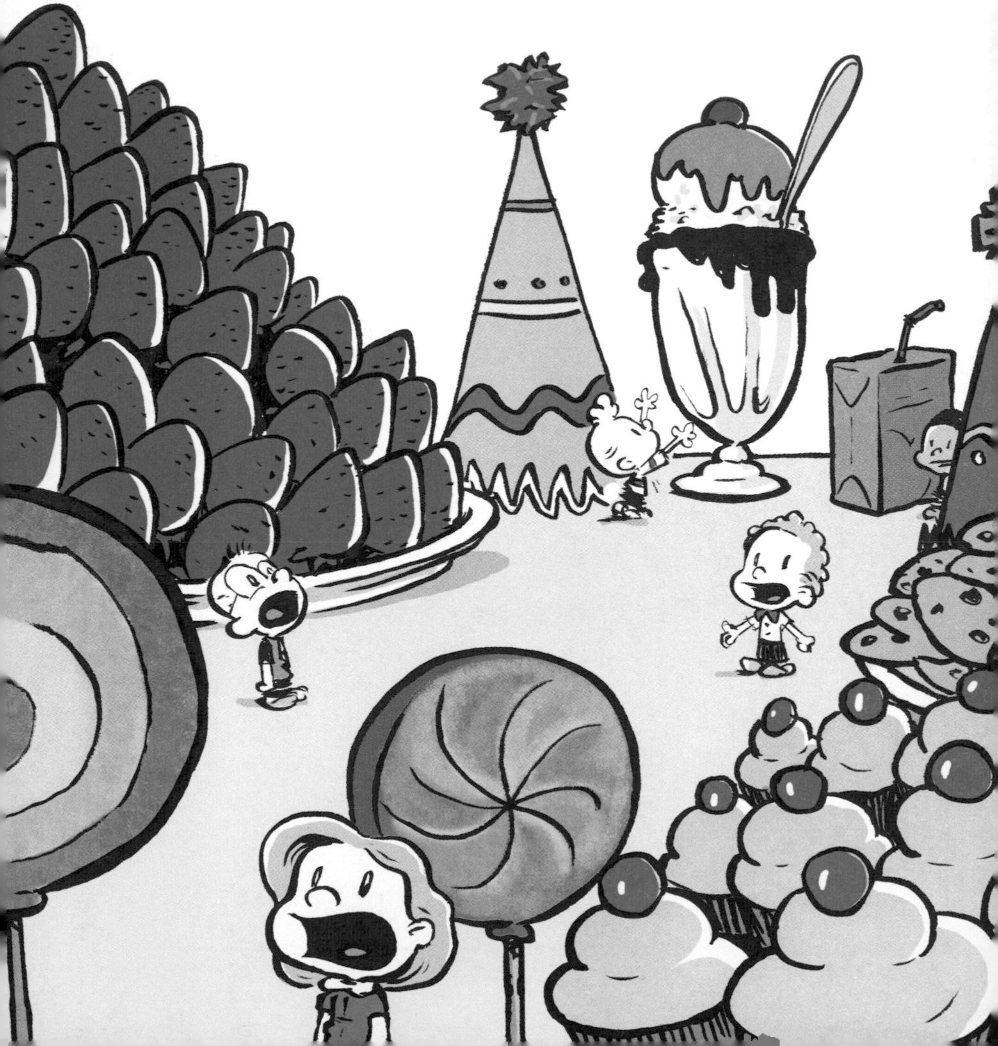

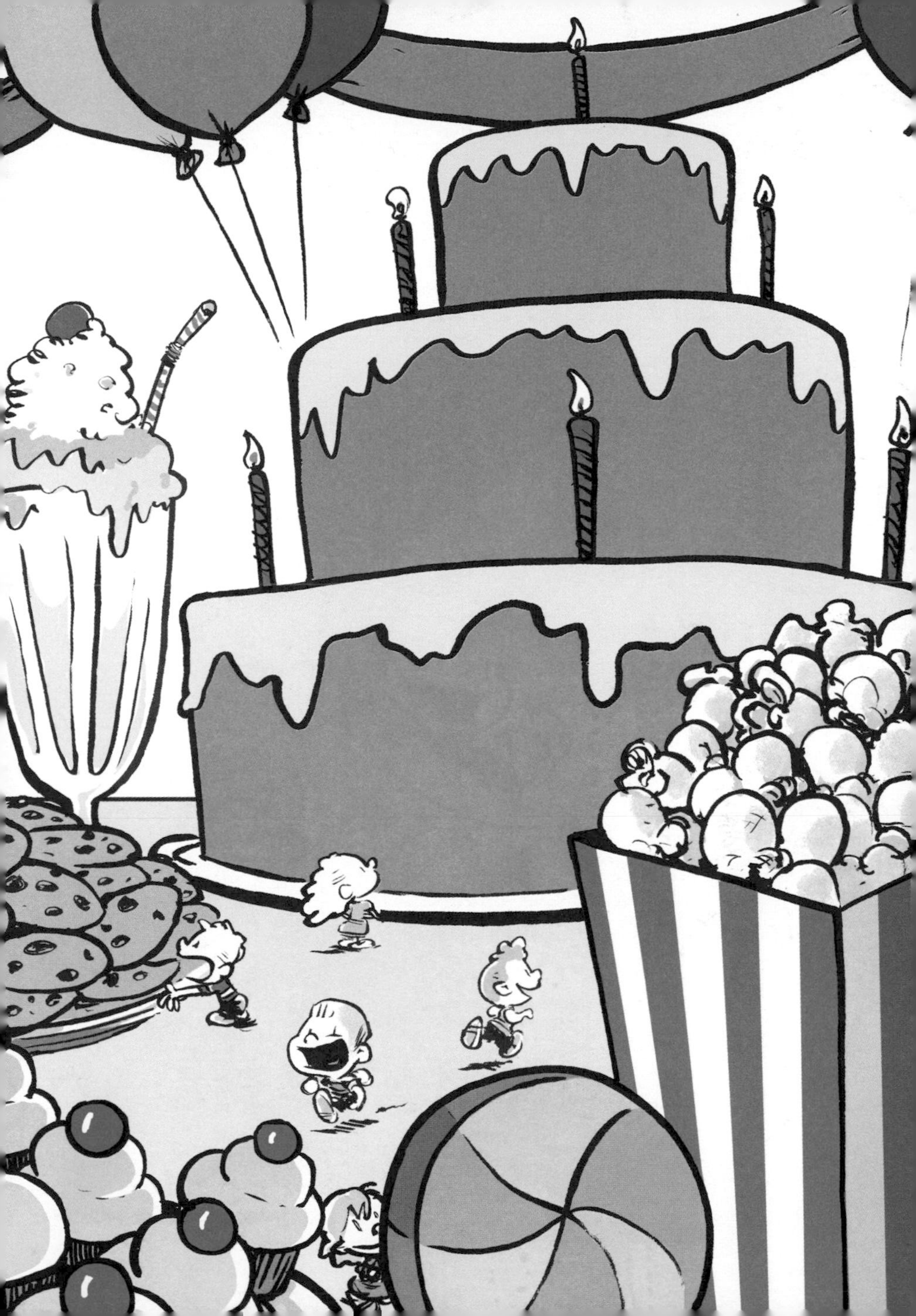

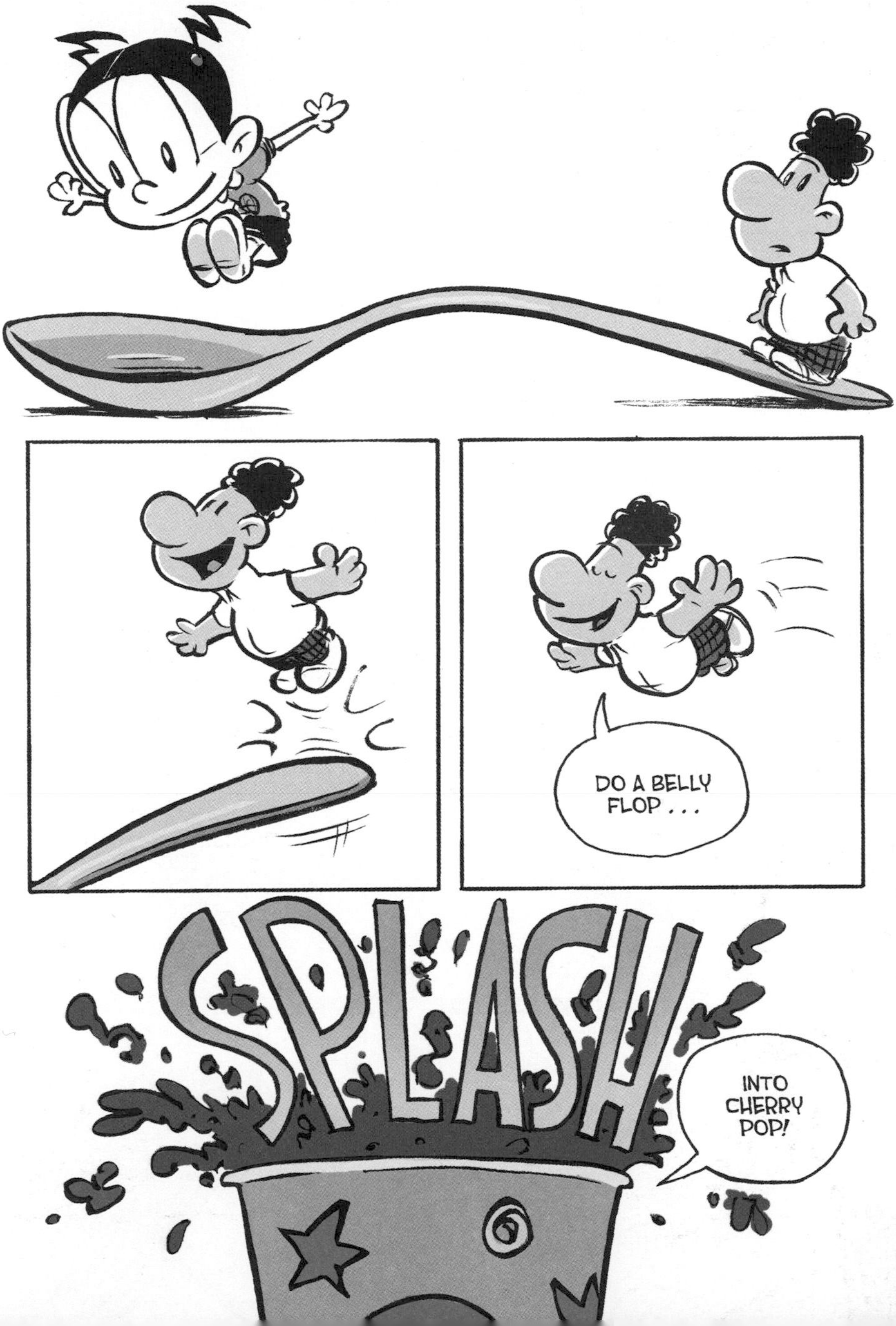
DO A BELLY FLOP . . .
SPLASH
INTO CHERRY POP!

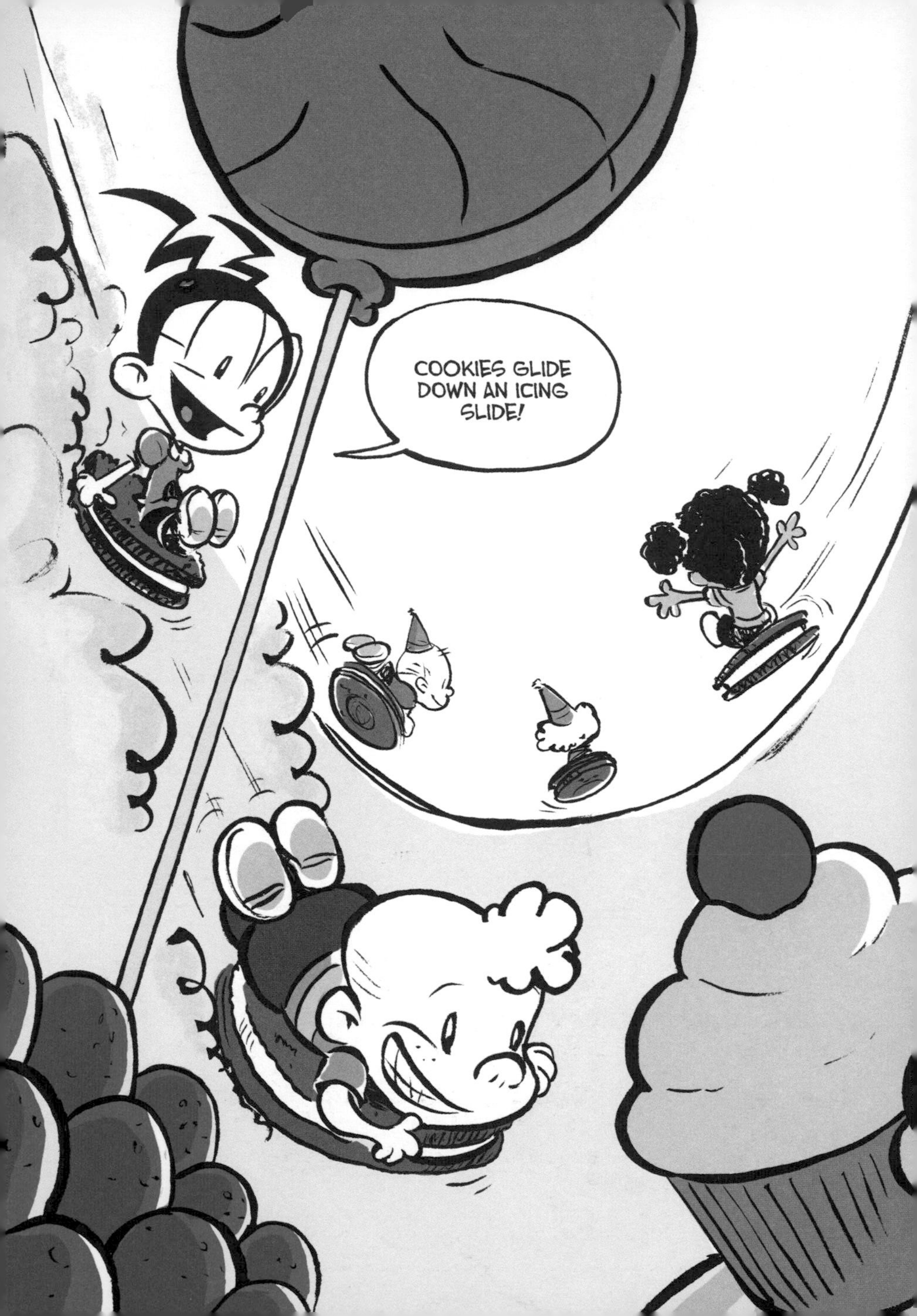
COOKIES GLIDE DOWN AN ICING SLIDE!

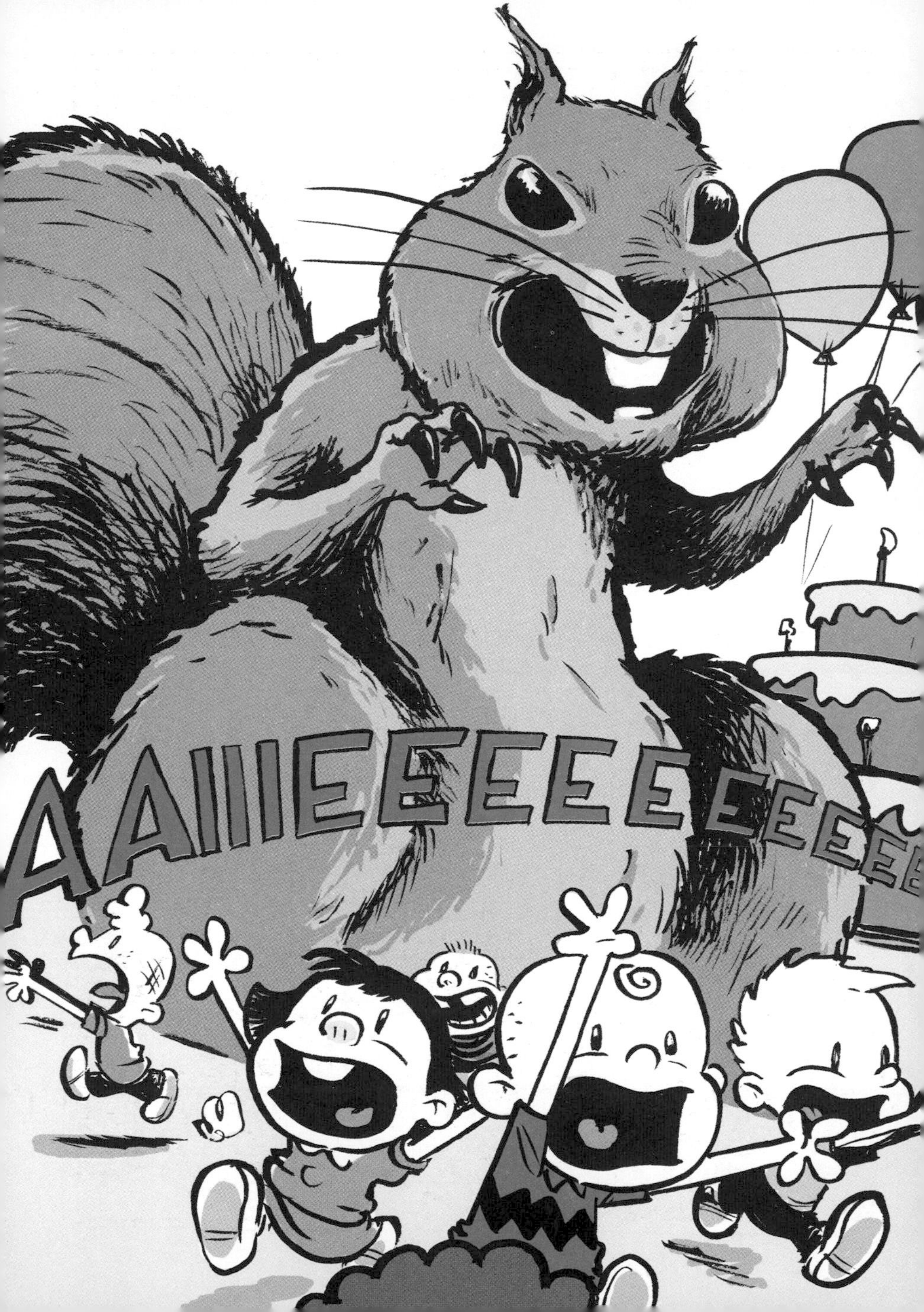
AAIIIEEEEEEEEEE

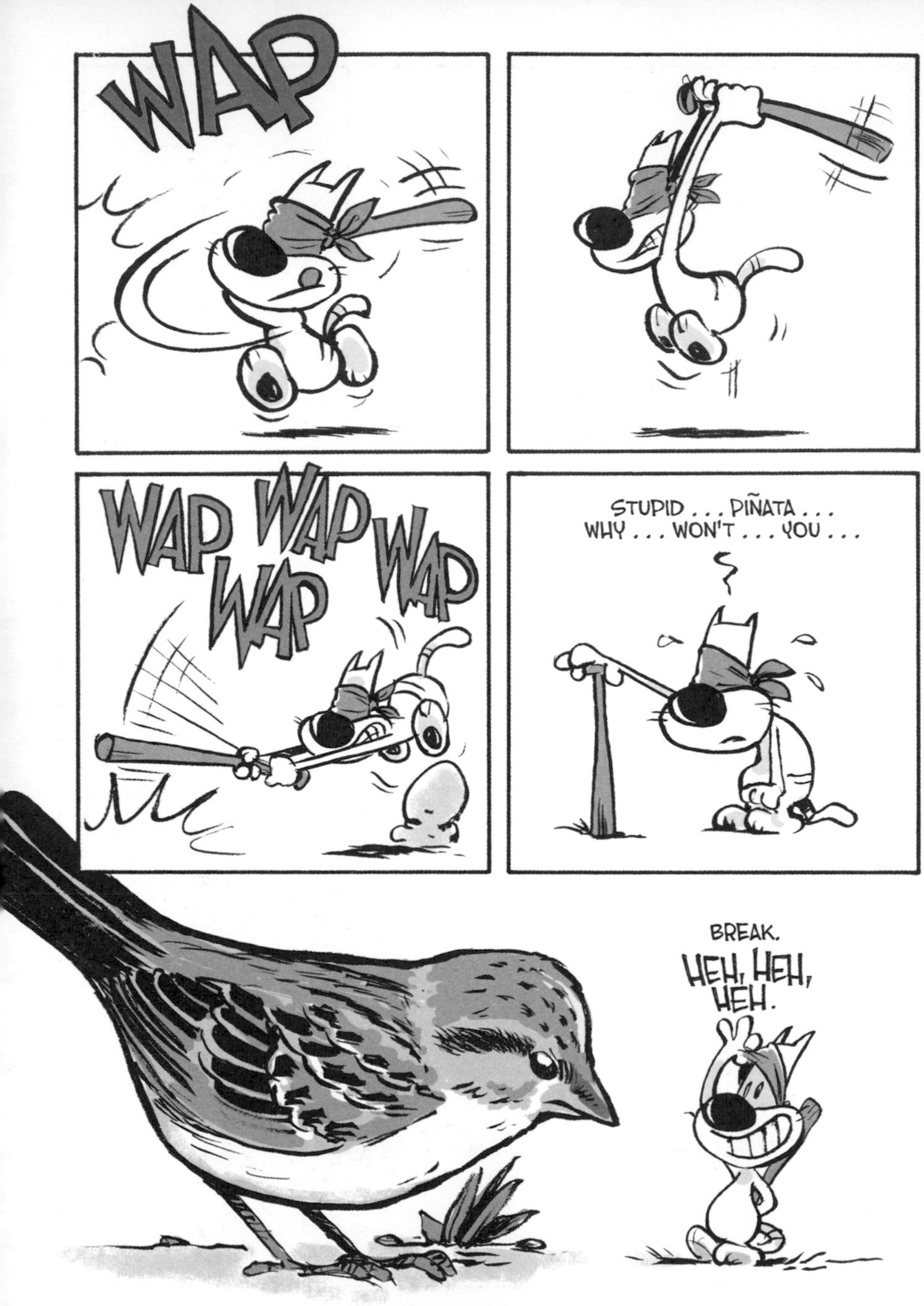
WAP
WAP WAP WAP WAP
STUPID . . . PIÑATA . . .
WHY . . . WON'T . . . YOU . . .
BREAK.
HEH, HEH, HEH.

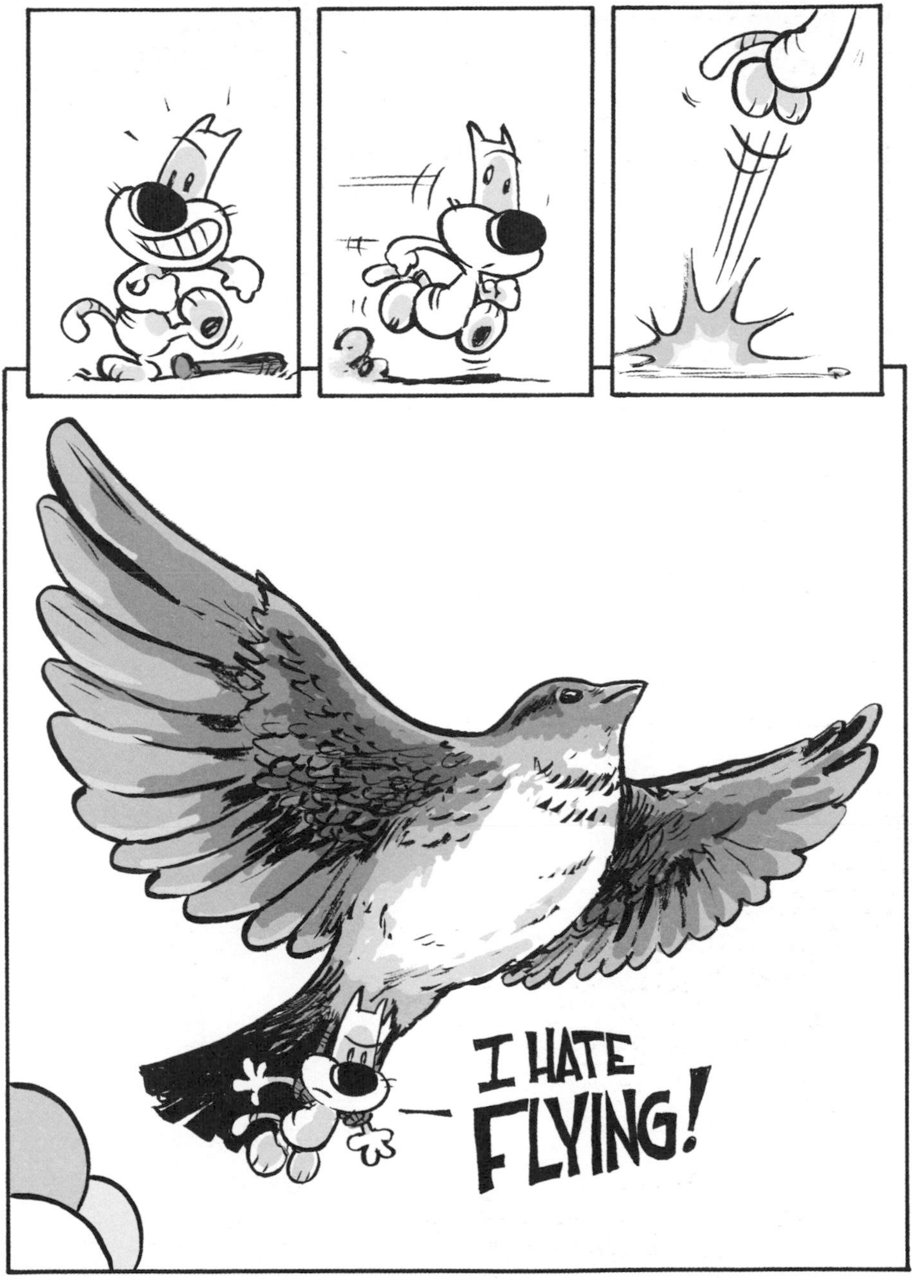
I HATE FLYING!

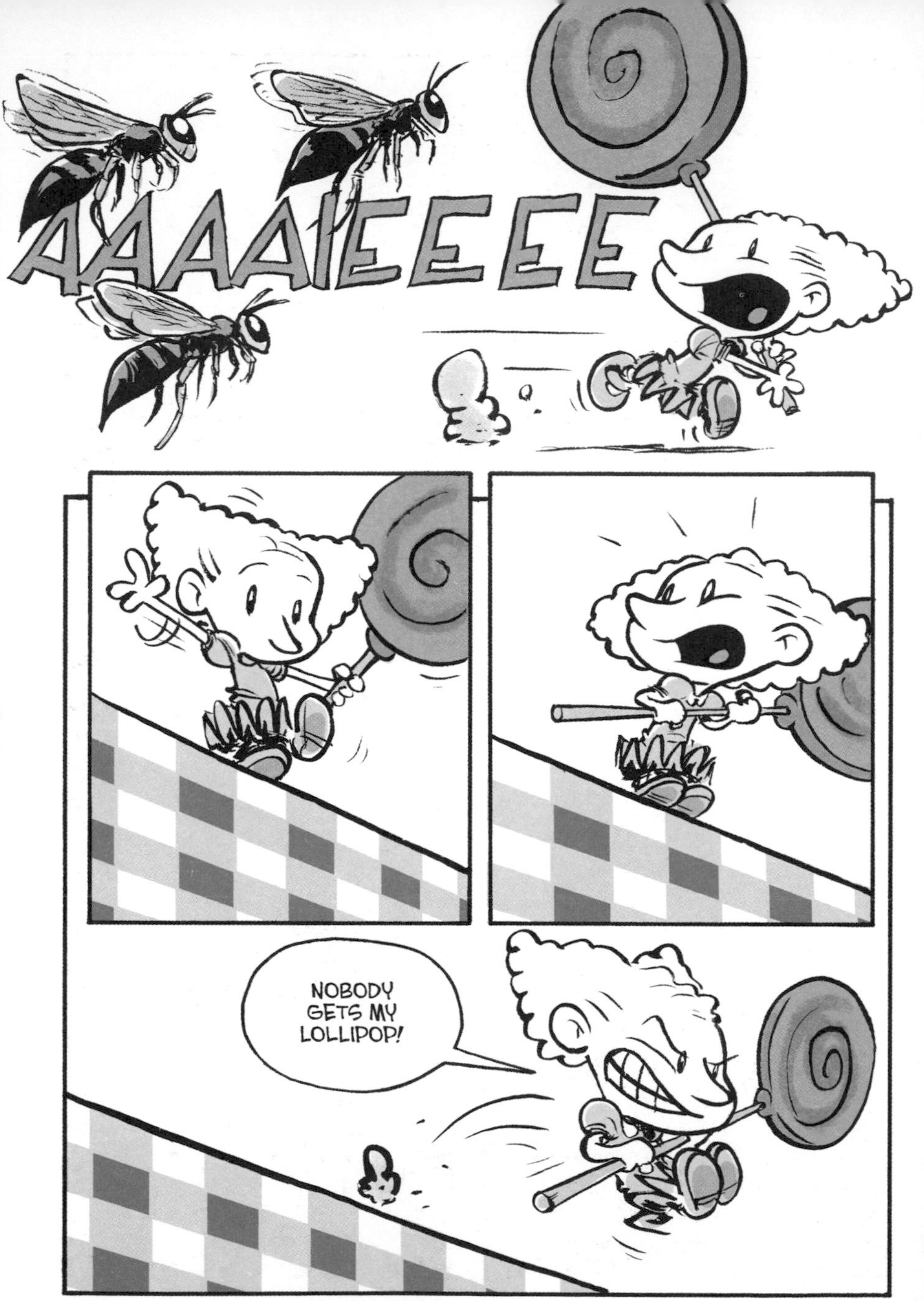
AAAAIEEEEE
NOBODY GETS MY LOLLIPOP!

83

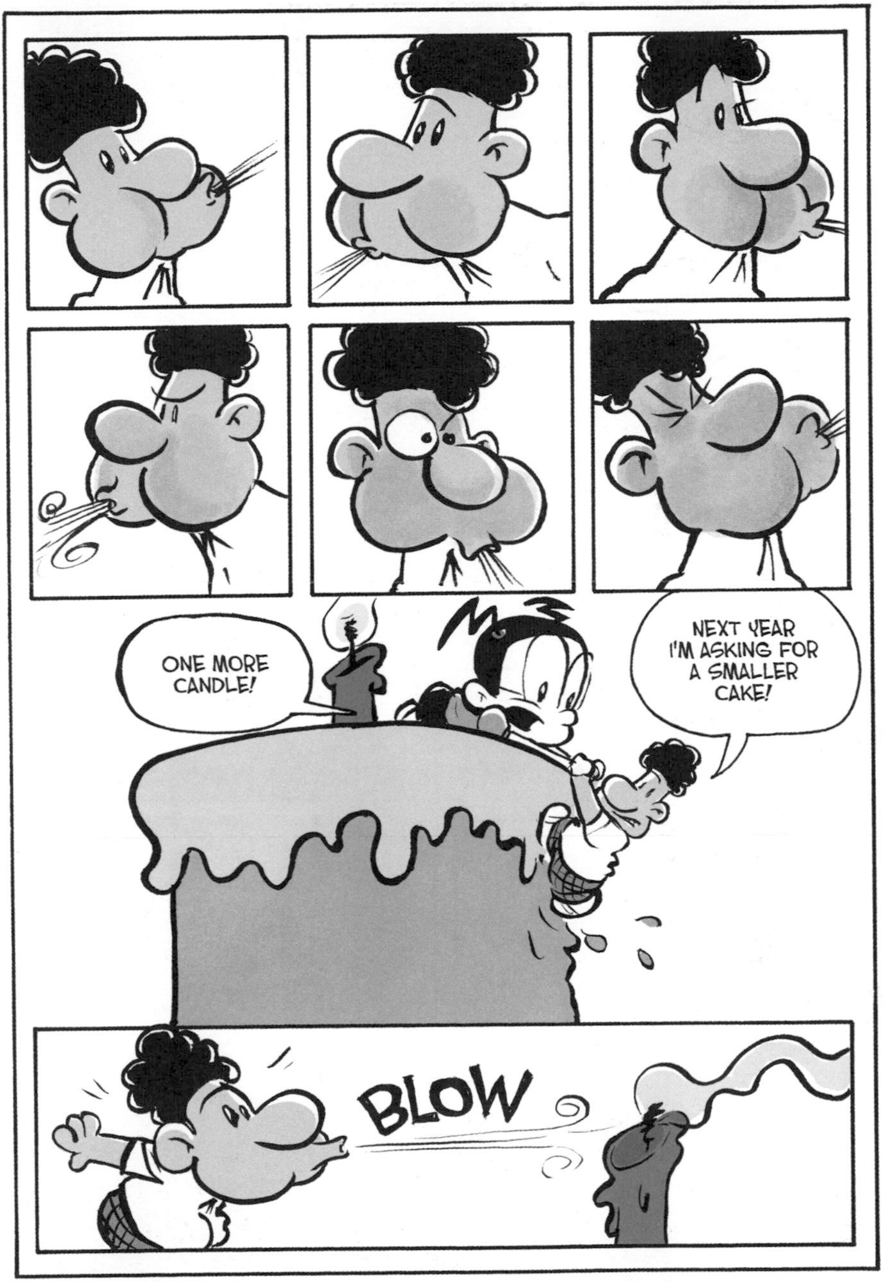
ONE MORE CANDLE!
NEXT YEAR I'M ASKING FOR A SMALLER CAKE!
BLOW

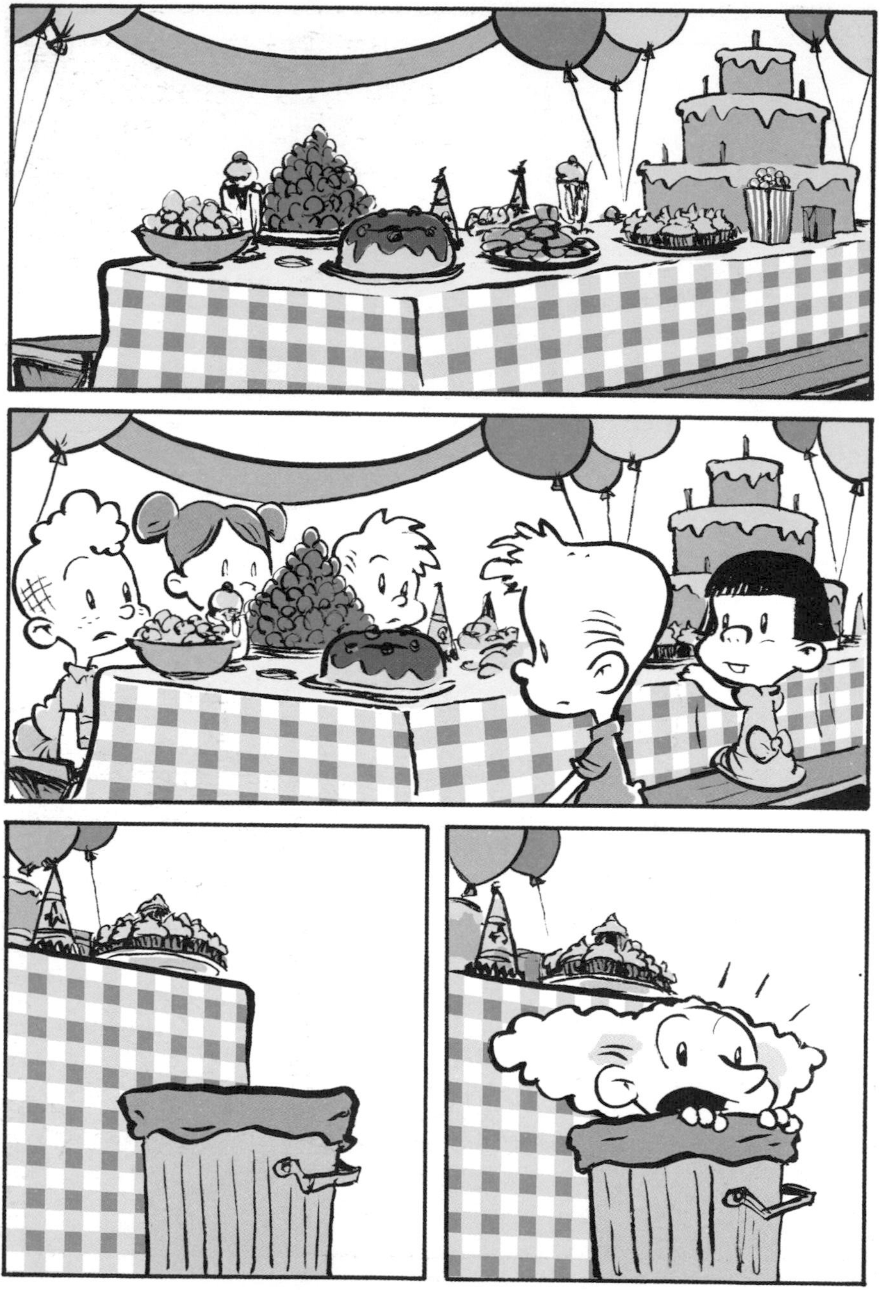

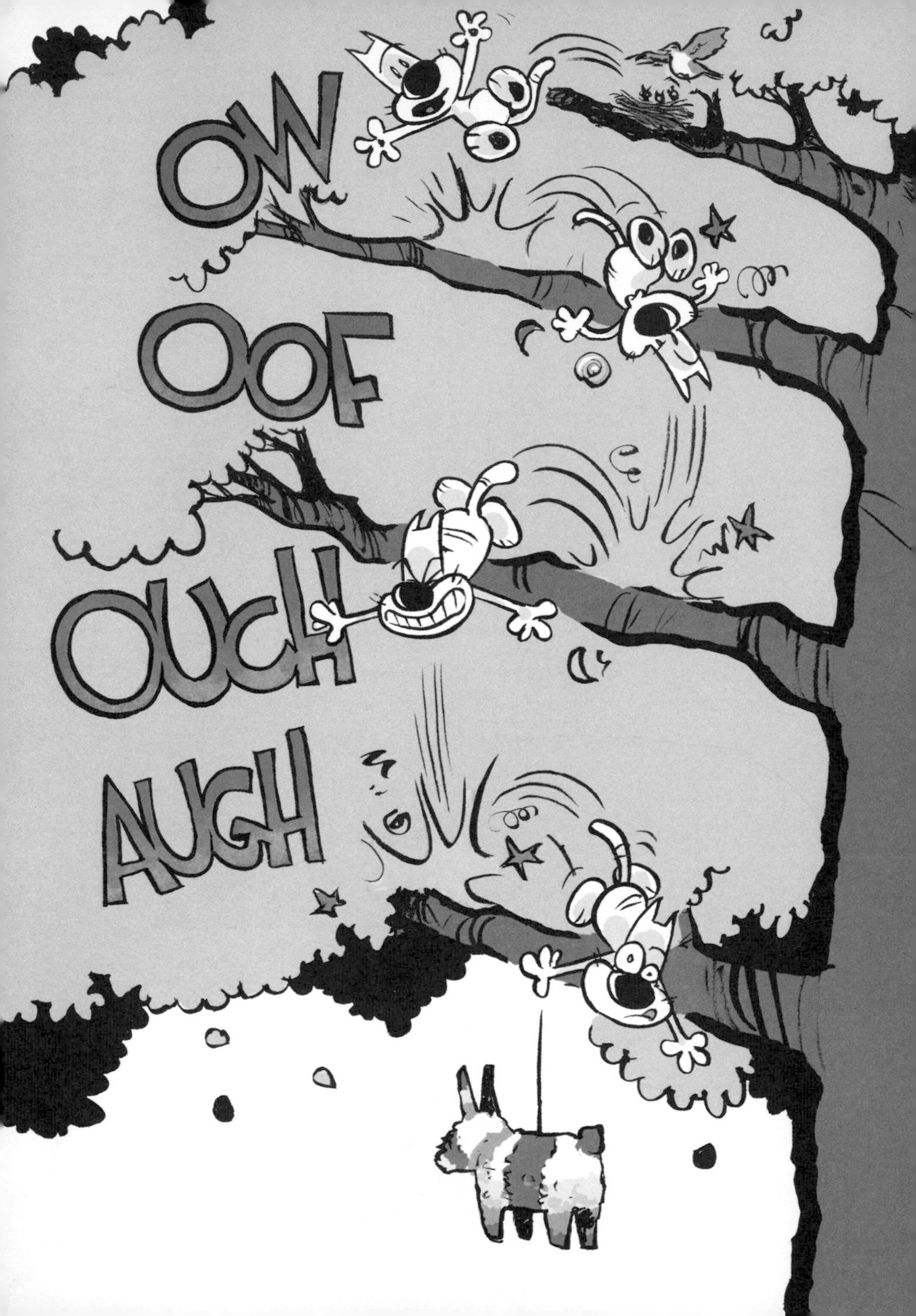
OW
OOF
OUCH
AUGH

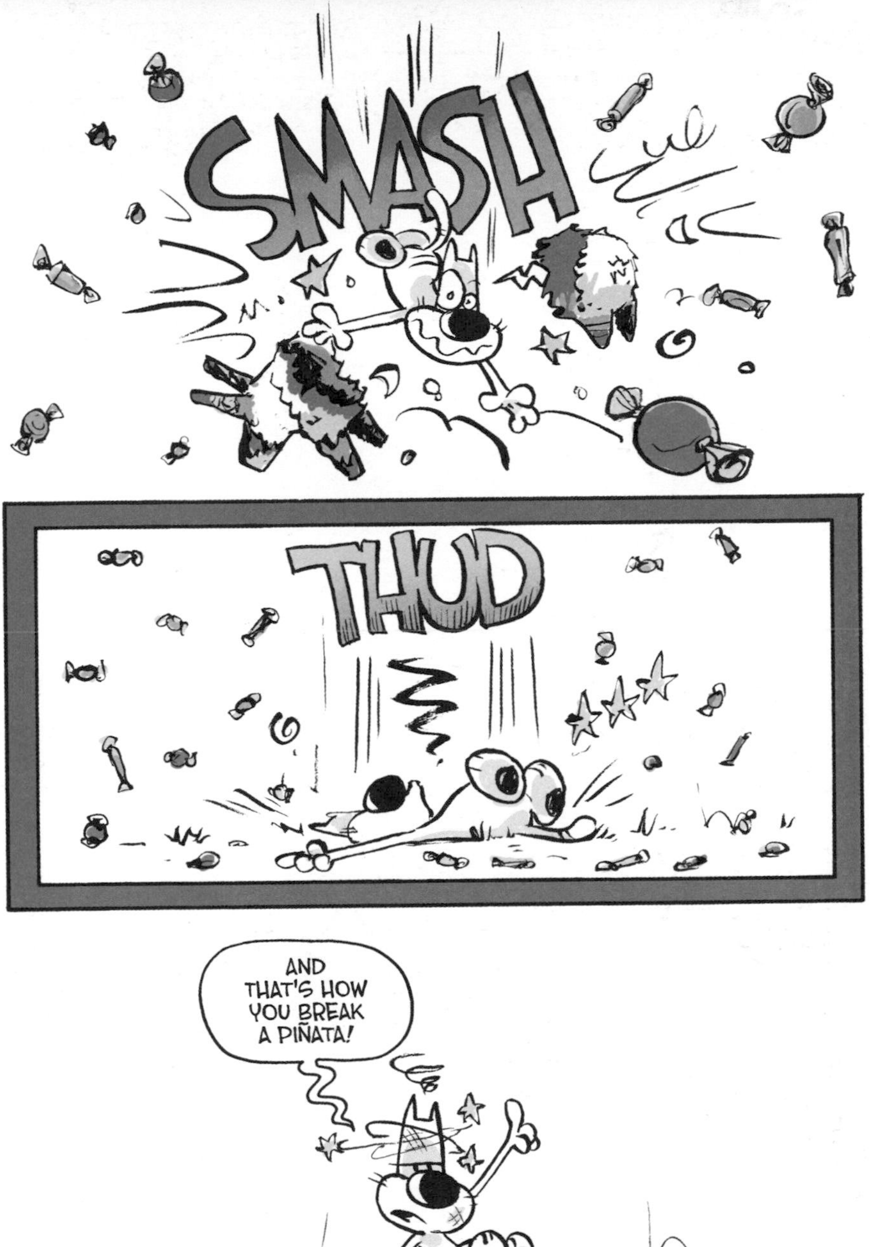
SMASH
THUD
AND THAT'S HOW YOU BREAK A PIÑATA!

93

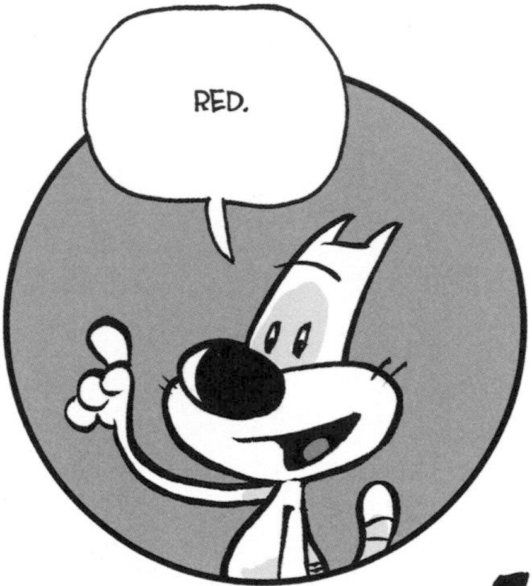
RED.

The End!

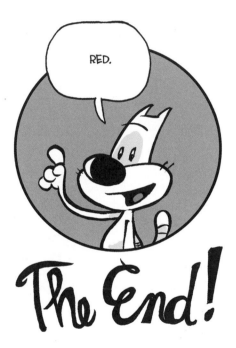

Getting to KNOW FRANK CAMMUSO

FRANK LIKES
1. SPENDING TIME WITH HIS FAMILY
2. PIZZA (ALL KINDS)
3. MAKING COMICS
4. READING COMICS (WHEN HE GETS A CHANCE)

FRANK DISLIKES
1. TUNA FISH
2. MAYONNAISE (ALL KINDS)
3. SHOVELING THE DRIVEWAY
4. BULLIES

FUN FACT: DID YOU KNOW THAT FRANK CAMMUSO ONCE GOT SICK AFTER DRINKING A SLUSHEE?

SPECIAL THANKS TO . . .

Ngoc and Khai, Kathy Leonardo, Nancy Iacovelli, Tom Peyer, Judy Hansen, Charlie Kochman, Maggie Lehrman, Sara Edward Corbett, Katie Fitch, Chad Beckerman, and finally to Hart Seely and Janice Whitcraft, who always enjoy a big party.

For more fun stuff about Salem & Whammy check out my website at . . .
www.cammuso.com